Be blessed,

What people are saying...

Every once in a great while, a book comes along that has the power to dramatically impact how people see the world so that after experiencing it, their lives are forever changed for the better. Dr. Joe Rubino's *The Seven Blessings* is one such book. This is a book that our world is currently calling for. Read this enchanting fable, discover the blessings and lessons that will enrich your life, and be the source of the change that will save our world.

Jack Canfield, Co-author of the Best-selling *Chicken Soup for the Soul®* series and *The Success Principles*

What are the secrets to being continually empowered to live your life full out, with passion and positive expectation, to effectively manage your negative self-talk and to be inspired to realize your dream life? Dr. Joe Rubino's *The Seven Blessings* is an uplifting, inspirational fable that will put you squarely on the journey to uncovering your own life's blessings, manifesting your greatest gifts, and living your life purpose. I give it my highest recommendation!

John Assaraf, New York Times Best-selling Author of *The Answer* and *Having It All* Featured in *The Secret.* CEO, OneCoach www.onecoach.com

What are the true secrets to living a life overflowing with blessings and void of resignation and regrets? You'll want to read master story-teller Dr. Joe Rubino's *The Seven Blessings* for the most entertaining fable I've ever read that provides life-changing insights into what it takes to be maximally happy, at peace, and empowered to live your best life.

Ron Tippe, Creative Empowerment Coach, Film Producer, *Shrek, Space Jam,* and *Everyone's Hero*

Dr. Joe Rubino's *The Seven Blessings* is an enchanting fable that is as entertaining as it is enlightening. Incorporating the blessings into your life will bring you greater joy, fulfillment, abundance, and peace of mind. I highly recommend the entire Trilogy of Light series.

Marci Shimoff, NY Times Best-selling author, *Happy for No Reason* and *Chicken Soup for the Woman's Soul*

Dr. Joe has done it again in his newest work, *The Seven Blessings: A Fable about the Secrets to Living Your Best Life.* In this long awaited prequel to *The Legend of the Light-Bearers* and *The Magic Lantern,* we are treated to a fable that reveals the seven blessings that could save the world…not just the fictional world of Joe[1]s making but arguably the real world we participate in every day.

The story's heroine, Nena learns the power of forgiveness together with the principles that lead to peace, abundance, harmony, happiness and fulfillment. This is an adventure story that yields tremendous insights into one's own self-imposed limitations and the way to release them. Follow Nena and you may find she mirrors much of what all of us hope and dream while she vanquishes the fears and doubts most of us have likewise experienced.

A must read from a man that genuinely knows both how to tell an outstanding story and how to motivate others to do and be their best!

Eldon Taylor, New York Times Best-selling author of *Choices and Illusions, Mind Programming* and *What Does That Mean?*

Do you want to learn the secrets to living a happy, abundant, fulfilled, at-peace life? Sometime just reading a fascinating fiction tale can open your mind to a new world of non-fiction possibilities. Dr. Joe Rubino has written just such a tale. Your answers could be found in *The Seven Blessings.*

Robert G. Allen, Author of *The One Minute Millionaire* and *Cash in a Flash*

If you are ready to attract abundance, meaningful relationships, joy, peace of mind, and fulfillment into your life, master story-teller and personal development expert Dr. Joe Rubino's *The Seven Blessings* is the book that will support these miracles to appear. If you read just one book this year, make this the one!

Bill Bartmann,
The Billionaire Business Coach

Our world is at a critical point in time. We can choose a future of love, joy, peace and prosperity or we can choose to focus on the negative aspects of our world and continue to accelerate that energy that can create more of what we don't want as a collective. Dr. Joe Rubino's *The Seven Blessings* is a fascinating tale that offers the antidote to any energy ailments we may seem to have as a collective. This important book will educate, entertain, and delight you while inspiring you to live with a newfound spiritual awareness that can impact the lives of others. It's a book you'll want to share with everyone you love.

Sharon Wilson, Founder and
Chief Inspiration Officer
CoachingFromSpirit.com

THE SEVEN BLESSINGS

A Fable about the Secrets to Living Your Best Life

By Dr. Joe Rubino

The Legends of Light Trilogy Series

The Seven Blessings
A Fable about the Secrets to Living Your Best Life

By Dr. Joe Rubino

Vision Works Publishing
First Edition Copyright @ 2011
By Dr. Joe Rubino

Published by Vision Works Publishing
(888) 821-3135 Fax: (630) 982-2134
VisionWorksBooks@email.com

Manufactured in the United States of America

ISBN 0-9728840-7-6 ISBN 13: 978-097288407-5
Library of Congress Catalog Card Number: 2010933813
10 9 8 7 6 5 4 3 2 1

Contents

About the Author

Dr. Joe Rubino, CEO of The Center for Personal Reinvention, http://www.CenterForPersonalReinvention.com, is acknowledged as one of the world's foremost experts on the topic of elevating self-esteem. He is a life-changing personal development and success coach on how to restore self-esteem, achieve business success, maximize joy and fulfillment in life and increase productivity. He is known for his groundbreaking work in personal and leadership development, building effective teams, enhancing listening and communication skills, life and business coaching and optimal life planning.

His 10 best selling books and 5 audio programs are available in 23 languages and in 53 countries and include:

- *The Self-Esteem Book: The Ultimate Guide to Boost the Most Underrated Ingredient for Success and Happiness in Life.* http://www.SelfEsteemSystem.com
- *The Success Code, Books I & II*
- *The Magic Lantern: A Fable about Leadership, Personal Excellence, and Empowerment*
- *The Legend of the Light-Bearers: A Fable about Personal Reinvention and Global Transformation*

Dr. Joe offers powerful personal and group coaching to support business success and life fulfillment. To contact him, call 888-821-3135 or email:

DrJoe@CenterForPersonalReinvention.com

Learn more about his life-changing work in championing people to restore their self-esteem at http://www.TheSelfEsteemBook.com and receive FREE the insightful audio program *7 Steps to Soaring Self-Esteem* and a FREE subscription to *The Success Achievers' Club*...a $129 Value!

Dr. Joe's *Legends of Light Trilogy* includes *The Magic Lantern, The Legend of the Light-Bearers,* and *The Seven Blessings.* All are currently in development as full length feature films.

Dedication

For my mother, Freda Rubino, 1930 – 2010, one of the true blessings of my life.

Joe Rubino

Acknowledgments

To my wife and partner, Janice, for her continuous love, encouragement, and belief in me

To my family for their unconditional love and support

To my friend and business partner, Jim Blakemore, for his commitment to championing our work in the world

To my friend and producer, Michael Lasky, for his brilliant work in supporting our shared vision to impact the lives of millions

To my gifted animator and designer, Cliff Schinkel, for bringing my characters to life through his art

To our talented IMI team who has taken on the vision of bringing the *Legends of Light* trilogy to the silver screen

To my editor, Evelyn Howell, for her insights and suggestions that have contributed to making the trilogy a richer experience

To those readers committed to the process of being their best and contributing their gifts to the world and living their life purposes with passion and contribution

Chapter 1

The Discovery

A cold, soaking rain fell upon the young girl's shoulders, streams of water cascading down through the fine strands of her strawberry blond hair in a torrent that brought a shiver to her petite athletic frame. She could see the steam rising from the tears in the dress she had so proudly donned in honor of the Builders' Award ceremony just a few hours before. How things had changed in the course of one evening!

As she adeptly made her way through the trees

along the ancient forest path that few (if any) had traversed in many a year, she stopped to wonder if she was shivering from the rain or from the certain fate that would await her and her family if she were caught by the hounds not so far behind her – and gaining - in pursuit.

"How could this be happening to *you*?" her shoulder companion asked her. Since the last Earth Change, Nena, like so many other humans, had become accustomed to the little gremlin-like character that clung to her shoulder, whispering advice non-stop into her ear. Since the cataclysm, almost everyone had a gremlin show up in the flesh to keep them protected from risking too much and to prevent them from feeling too self-confident. Gremlins bore a strong facial resemblance to their humans, but possessed diminutive and often grossly distorted bodies. Sure they kept their folks in line, but at what cost? Nena often wondered.

"Were you not descended from the noblest of stock? Were your ancestors not the ones responsible for the very founding and growth of what so many had called the greatest civilization ever to grace the planet's countenance?" her companion now demanded to know.

As the two now ran for their lives, the words of her great-grandmother Ohma haunted her. As they had dressed to attend what should have been the happiest of events, Ohma had confided, "Times have changed, my dear Nena. I have seen visions that our leaders have and will further betray the work that your great-great-grandfather Termaine began so many years ago. The same work that my son, Silvester and I devoted our lives to, the work that I thought would live on forever, well beyond our days."

Nena had wondered what Ohma had meant by those words, but the words added a bit more to the inner rage that fueled her gremlin's mistrust of others. Before she could ask Ohma to explain further, they were interrupted and whisked away to attend the ceremony.

Ohma was truly a legend. She was known to her people simply as "the Auger," both for her gift of prophesy and for the wisdom and love she embodied and had shared so readily over just shy of the past three centuries with the people who loved and respected her. People marveled at how Ohma was one of the very few who did not need to listen to the constant chatter of a companion of her own, unlike the majority of the inhabitants of the World Above. Ohma's grandfather had founded their civilization and now not only was his legacy in danger, but the very lives of all his living descendants as well!

As she brushed by a thorny briar, it scratched Nena's arm, causing blood to pool up and mix with the sweat and rain that now ran freely down the nape of her neck. "You, clumsy fool!" her gremlin barked into Nena's ear. "Watch where you're going!"

Yes, she knew that she was fleeing for her life. But even more important to her was her need to warn the others of her discovery and the impending peril it represented to their entire world. She took this obligation very personally. After all, her companion reminded her all too frequently, "You must see that the traitors are punished! We must bring these conspirators to justice! Don't forget: men can't be trusted!"

"I know, I know! Enough already," Nena murmured under her strained breathing.

From the time she could first understand the spoken word, she had learned of her family's courageous commitment to leadership. Now in her 16th year, she knew full well that great challenges called for great leadership. As she ran, she could not help but hear her companion wonder aloud to her if this would be her opportunity to carry on the family tradition and see that justice be done, or if instead it would be her darkest hour.

"You're probably not up to the crisis at hand," her companion reminded her yet again.

The last of more than 2000 attendees filed into the Great Hall located on the first level of the Septropolis. The long-awaited gala event was by invitation only and anyone living either within the Septropolis or the World Above who was someone of importance was on the guest list. Ohma was actually surprised to receive an invitation to attend. She knew that her strong opposition to the changes that were being proposed by the Council members now in control of the governing body had made her persona non grata as far as they were concerned. Ohma knew that they concealed many secrets from her and figured that those in charge wanted to keep an eye on her and that was likely the only reason inviting her.

Some 40 minutes before, just as they were about to enter the Great Hall, Nena had excused herself, saying only that she would be back in a few minutes and would meet her great-grandmother inside the function room. Knowing Nena's inherent curiosity and strong-willed nature, Ohma had agreed. But now, as more and more time elapsed, Ohma's concern increased with each passing minute.

As she now waited for the event to get started, Ohma looked around the festively appointed ballroom. On the walls hung pictures of the many leaders who had recently risen to power. To Ohma's left hung a portrait of Zuavas, the newly appointed leader of the Council, with the inscription "Integrity" written beneath it. A bit further along the same wall hung the portrait of Chacum, now second in command.

The inscription "Vision" accompanied it. As Ohma looked around the room, she could see several other Council members with such labels as "Courage," "Leadership," and "Commitment" framing their likenesses. "The irony is enough to make one ill," she muttered under her breath. Conspicuously absent was her own portrait, along with those of the courageous and dedicated Council leaders such as Cyrit, Jonas, and Nanse with whom Ohma had worked tirelessly for years to promote the common good.

The lights dimmed and one of the newer Council appointees began his introduction of the evening's first speaker. "In the very brief time that I have known this individual, the man I am about to introduce to you has already become a legend within the Septropolis. He is a visionary leader who is not afraid to shake things up because of his commitment to you all. He is not afraid to make the tough decisions that will protect us from any threats that may be posed by the undesirable elements of our world. His wisdom and foresight will guide the people of our great city now and long into the future. Please join me in welcoming our great leader, Zuavas!"

The band played a jubilant march as the attendees rose to their feet in wild applause. After a few minutes, Zuavas quieted the crowd and spoke, "Thank you, thank you! It is a great honor to be here before you this evening as we celebrate the grand accomplishment of the Septropolis!"

The crowd rose again to their feet and their enthusiastic applause resumed.

Motioning the crowd to quiet down, Zuavas continued, "As you know, the construction of our great subterranean city has been decades in the making. Hewn from solid rock, our city can withstand the direct impact of our enemies' fiercest weapons. This city will make us invincible against all who oppose us! In combination with the awesome new technology that our scientists are developing right now, even as I speak, we will possess the ferocious power to dominate the world and annihilate all who oppose our domination!"

The power-hungry crowd went wild. They chanted "Zuavas, Zuavas, Zuavas!"

Zuavas said, “We have already begun to take steps to silence our adversaries, to rid our world of undesirable beings, and destroy any who would interfere with our God-appointed authority to rule with an iron fist!”

Ohma could see that the crowd had quickly determined that it was in their best interests to support this authoritarian ruler rather than risk his wrath by opposing him. She knew that he was baiting her and knew full well what would happen to her if she opposed him but she decided that she could stay silent no longer.

“But what of the rights of all people? Are we not a people of laws? Have we not a tradition of honoring others and respecting diversity?” she shouted in reply.

“This is the very sort of insolence that makes a people weak!” Zuavas shot back. “Arrest this traitor now!” Chacum, Zuavas’ second in command ordered.

Within seconds, several guards pounced upon the wise leader that so many had once loved and respected and dragged her out of the hall.

As Nena ascended the wooded path of the foothills leading to the Great Mountain, she could see the hooded figures, cloaked in black on horseback in the distance, still relentless in their pursuit. She guessed that they trailed her by about a mile. Surely, if the going through the brush were not so difficult, they would have caught her long ago. Unfortunately the hounds were not experiencing quite as much difficulty.

"They'll be upon us soon," she heard her companion's voice mutter under her breath. "If you hadn't been so clumsy and dropped your water gourd, they would have never discovered us in the corridor of the Forbidden Wing!"

"Shut up!" Nena answered back, now tiring of the grremlin's voice.

Do I sense the resignation other mortals would have likely succumbed to long ago?" her shoulder companion added, obviously needing to get in the last word.

Nena's path soon flattened out and she made the most of the opportunity to pick up speed. The hounds were gaining on her and there wasn't much she could do about it. As she glanced back to gauge the progress of the hounds, a low-hanging limb struck her across the neck. As she fell to the ground, she realized that they would be upon her in seconds. As her body flipped from the jolt of the tree limb, her head hit a log and she was unconscious in an instant, even before her companion had a chance to scold her for her foolish mistake.

Chapter 2

The World Below

Nena sat up, ready for a fight, startled from the shocking sensation of a cold compress across her still-throbbing forehead. In the dim light that filtered in from a crack in the cave ceiling somewhere high above her head, she could see the vague outline of a young handsome man stooping before her. His shoulder-length straight black hair hung over kind brown eyes and a smiling face. In the corner of the cave was another man, busily preparing a sling for her arm.

"Who are you? What do you want from her?" Nena's companion demanded.

"And where am I?" Nena blurted out, expecting to be in the clutches of her captors, rather than in the hands of a caring nurse and his assistant.

"We want nothing of you but to help you. I am Plabius and this is Ishim," he said with a tender smile nodding in the direction of his companion. "You are safe here. Do not fret. Last night we saw you running from your pursuers and when you were knocked unconscious, we hurriedly whisked you away to this subterranean shelter."

"But how could that be?" Nena interrupted with a puzzled stare. "I recall that as I fell, the hounds were seconds away from tearing me apart!"

"They're probably lying! Remember the rules

about men: they can't be trusted and they abandon you when you need them most!" the companion warned.

"Since the Earth Change, we have been blessed with many extraordinary gifts. I used my powers to turn the hounds into glass before swooping down to carry you away," Plabius answered defensively.

"Swooping?" Nena queried.

"Yes, our people developed the gift of flight in the Earth Change." Plabius attempted to change the subject, obviously not totally comfortable with his strange talents. "I have been dressing your wounds and sitting with you all night long. They will not find you here. It is now morning in the World Above and they have given up their search...at least for now."

"Where are your companions?" Nena asked, expecting Plabius and his friend to share in the company of their own gremlins.

"In the Inner World, the Earth Change brought us many surprises, but gremlin companions were not among them. I'm afraid, that change only affected those of your kind in the World Above," Plabius answered.

As Plabius turned to grab a fresh cold compress, Nena caught a glimpse of wings protruding from his rugged shoulders. She turned toward Ishim and saw that he too possessed wing-like structures on his back.

"Who, er, I mean, what are you?" she whispered in puzzlement, still not fully trusting her caregivers as she heeded her companion's warnings.

"We are mutants living here in the Inner World, a world you likely know nothing about!" Ishim interjected in a tone that Nena took for either sadness or apology. "The dark forces brought about the Earth Change that turned us into a race of freaks," he continued angrily.

"Before last evening, you would have been correct in your assumption that this would be news to me," Nena countered. "The events of the last 12 hours are just now beginning to make more sense."

"You *know* about us?" Plabius uttered back in shocked disbelief.

"Last evening, I attended the Builders' Awards.

You know, to honor the architects, designers, and construction workers who created the great seven-level subterranean city they call the Septropolis. After a while I grew restless with the stuffiness of the ceremony and decided to take a walk around the compound. Besides, my great-grandmother had mentioned something to me that made my companion and me suspicious that some mischief was taking place. I stumbled upon a meeting that was going on in one of the rooms on the Forbidden Wing of the compound. My suspicious curiosity got the best of me I suppose, that being the "Forbidden Wing" and all. I overheard a group of men speaking about "the problem" and how they were going about "eliminating it." I soon learned that secret tests that had been conducted years ago under the Great Hall had resulted in an opening into the Inner World, as they called it. They spoke of some new races of "undesirables" that had sprung up in this strange new world with its own atmosphere where it rained underground. The problem they were wrestling with was how they could go about "exterminating *all* the “vermin” that resulted from what they called the last Earth Change. One of the men spoke of a site that had been created deep within the subterranean city to “deal with the freaks” and any who accidently had learned about them.”

“Yes, I guess you know by now that we are two of those freaks,” Ishim sighed. “I can’t tell you how mad that makes me!”

Plabius interrupted, “A number of decades ago, some of the scientists and politicians in your world decided to conduct secret underground tests of a powerful, new energy technology. They wanted to develop this technology to gain awesome power over all who opposed them. They conducted a series of experiments deep in the Earth, under the seven-story underground city that had been created in the bedrock as both a monument to their advanced civilization and a protective precaution they assumed would shelter them from any future enemy aggression.”

“Yes, my ancestors were the ones who originally envisioned that great subterranean city to serve the needs of future generations,” Nena offered. “The builders called that structure the Septropolis and were extremely proud of their accomplishment. The builders said it was the strongest, most impenetrable structure ever created by man. They said it was the successful model for more underground civilizations they wished to construct long into the future. My wise great-grandmother often commented that the builders distorted a concept that was originally intended only for the good of the people. The greedy leaders who have recently come to power saw the underground city as a means to line their pockets and prepare themselves to wage war on their neighbors so they could rule the world. It was during the award ceremony to honor these builders for this great accomplishment that I wondered off and discovered their dark and evil secret!" Nena added.

Ishim continued, "The trouble all began when they were unable to harness the fearsome power that their work with crystals unleashed. Apparently much work had been conducted by those seeking to develop the power to dominate all others with their new weapons. A rift was created between the earth plates during repeated tests beneath the Septropolis, and the Inner World you spoke of was expanded."

"You should have known they couldn't be trusted," Nena's companion whispered into her ear.

"It never ceases to amaze me about how people lie and betray you!" Nena fumed.

"You think it makes you angry!" Ishim added. "Look at how their greedy and careless actions affected us!"

"Are we in the Inner World now?" Nena wondered.

"We are in one of the vortex channels that communicate between the World Above and the Inner World below. Some of our people have used these channels to return to your world. There were originally more than 300 in existence. The corrupt Council members and their armies located most of these channels and blew them up to prevent more of our kind from going above. Many who had attempted to go above were apprehended. The detention sites you overhead discussions about are the places they were sent... to dispose of the vermin, as they call us. This particular vortex has remained hidden from the Council so far. But I fear they will discover it eventually and destroy it as well."

"Are there more, ahem, like you?" Nena asked, not wanting to offend.

"Yes, I am one of the Sumarians. Many races were created by the energy unleashed from the last Earth Change."

"Were there additional Earth Changes?" Nena interjected.

"Yes, at least two more that we know about since the first one."

"Well, how can we just sit here, knowing that good people are being tortured and killed as we speak?" Nena raged.

"Calmdown, calmdown!" hercompanionwhispered.

"We can discuss a plan to take action soon, but first you must rest and regain your strength. When you have done so, I will ask that you tell us more of your story," Plabius invited. "Sleep and know you are safe here for now. You will need your strength soon enough."

With those words, Nena closed her eyes, tried to forget about the throbbing pain in her neck and arm, reminded herself that her new friends could be trusted, in spite of her companion's warnings to the contrary, and drifted back to a fitful sleep.

Chapter 3

The Rise of a Great Civilization

The light filtering down from the crack high above in the cave ceiling found its way to Nena's eyes, rousing her from her nightmarish slumber. Plabius and Ishim had arisen a short time before and were busily preparing a makeshift breakfast.

"Did you get much sleep?" Ishim asked.

"You tossed and turned all night," Plabius added.

"I still can't believe how deceitful people can be. I hope my groaning didn't keep you up!" Nena apologized.

"We can sleep through just about anything!" Ishim chuckled. "Have some seed cakes and tea and regain your strength."

"Thank you, I am famished!" Nena offered with a smile, thankfully accepting breakfast from her new friends.

"Do you feel up to sharing your story with us?" Plabius invited.

"It is the least I could do to thank you for saving my life, but I'm still feeling a bit dazed from my fall." Nena apologized.

"With the prior Earth Change, we developed a type of telepathic power," Plabius explained. "If you are willing, just by touching your forehead, we can project your thoughts upon the cave wall. Would that be okay with you?"

"Don't trust them, it could be dangerous," warned Nena's companion.

"Okay, quiet now!" Nena scolded, returning her focus to her new friends.

"Why, that's amazing! I have the feeling that I am just beginning to learn of your peoples' many gifts and talents. Are you sure it's safe? How do I know I can trust you?"

"It's perfectly safe, I promise," Plabius assured.

"Okay then. That would be wonderful. I will trust you and welcome the experience!" Nena decided.

"Great! So, can we ask you some questions to get you started, if that's all right?" Ishim continued. "Your companion will be asleep during the entire process. You just might enjoy the respite!"

"Yes, of course, ask away," Nena agreed. "You're right. I do tire of her constant negative chatter at times."

"Well, one thing I've been wondering about is how you were even able to get access to the Forbidden Wing of the Septropolis' first level? I know that security there is awfully tight!"

Plabius placed his two hands with his fingers gently

touching on Nena's forehead. Instantly, they all viewed a projection in full color upon the wall of the cave.

"That's amazing!" Nena commented, watching intently as her thoughts sprang to life on the wall.

The three viewed the following scene: Nena and her great-grandmother Ohma, dressed in elegant evening dresses, approached the security checkpoint. Security passes hung from their necks and the guards scanned them and welcomed them graciously to enter.

"How did you get those?" Plabius wondered aloud.

The scene shifted to focus upon Ohma. They watched as the projection ran through a brief history of Nena's great-grandmother's life and accomplishments. They witnessed Ohma's rise to leadership, her partnership with the king, her creation of the Great Halls of Learning, her contributions to the people, and the great love and respect they demonstrated for her.

"Why, your great-grandmother is the Auger!" Ishim exclaimed.

"Even the Sumarians have heard of her! She is a

legend," Plabius marveled. "I've heard of her wisdom, leadership, and empathy for others on many occasions."

'Thank you, she would be pleased to know that you hold her contributions in high regard," Nena smiled, temporarily interrupting the projection.

"If you are related to the Auger then that must make you royalty too!" Ishim added.

The scene shifted to show the coronation of Nena's great-great-grandfather, King Termaine. He stood before a gathering of more people than Ishim and Plabius had ever seen assembled in one place at one time. The crowd cheered wildly. People cried with happiness. It became apparent that Termaine was greatly loved and admired by the people he served.

"So, tell us, how did he get to become king?" Ishim queried, interrupting the coronation scene.

"Well, as the story goes.... Are you sure you want to hear, I mean, see this?" Nena interrupted herself, not wanting to bore her companions.

"Yes!" "Yes!" they both said in unison. "This

is fascinating!"

The scene shifted to show a teen boy out picking wild mushrooms. Before long, it started to rain and the boy, who all guessed to be the young Termaine, dashed for cover, finding a slight crack in a nearby rocky ledge that led to a tunnel that went deep into the Earth. Termaine followed the tunnel for quite some time, finally coming to a cave. It was clear that the cave had not been inhabited for a long, long time. The scene showed the progression of time over the millenniums and the viewers realized that about 24,000 years had passed since it was last occupied. The cave was obviously deep under the Earth.

"That cave was probably located at about level six or seven of the Septropolis, I imagine," Plabius added.

"Yes, I suppose you are right!" Ishim concurred. "Let her finish!"

The three watched as Termaine lit a fire to keep warm with some material he found in the cave. Soon, clouds of smoke from the wood and other debris filled the cave. Coughing and trying to escape the smoke, Termaine climbed up on a ledge within the cave to enter a remote cavern. It was there on the wall that he first noticed an inscription.

"That looks like it says "I M I." Plabius observed.

Nena interrupted the scene with a comment to add clarity, "He took this inscription to mean "I am I, the proud, the competent, the self-confident and the capable." He went back to his people and established "I AM I" as his empowering rallying call. Throughout the land, he challenged people to believe in themselves, to let their inner magnificence show forth. This was particularly important because the evil and selfish tyrant Ikidluk ruled the land both in the World Above and in the Inner World with an iron hand."

"Great concept, but they've now gone too far, if you ask me! The current Council members have too much self-confidence for their own good!" Ishim huffed.

"It does appear they went overboard," Plabius agreed.

Nena was once again silent as the new scene unfolded. The three watched. "I, the great Ikidluk, hereby decree, from high on this hill that all my subjects are from this time forward to pay homage to me! I am your ruler, divinely appointed by God! You must obey my every command and never forget that without my guidance and mercy, you are lost and helpless!"

Scene after scene displayed the tyrant continually reminding the people about how lowly, worthless, and flawed they were. The three observed the hardship, suffering and despair that Ikidluk relentlessly brought upon his people.

"Wow, I had no idea what a tyrant he was!" Plabius offered. "So Termaine empowered the people instead!"

The scene from Nena's mind continued to unfold the tale she had been told on so many occasions. The three watched Termaine rally the people to oppose the tyrant's unjust laws. They watched as Termaine formed a sort of underground resistance.

Speaking before the masses, Termaine challenged, "I encourage you, my comrades, to engage in peaceful protests. I invite you *not* to turn over half of your harvest to this evil tyrant as is required by his unjust law. I challenge you to believe in yourselves! I encourage you to see that you are not dependent upon Ikidluk for your survival! You are magnificent and capable, all of you are! Do not give your power away to anyone, ever!"

"That must have gone over really great with Ikidluk!" Ishim surmised.

"You got that right!" Nena commented.

The scene shifted to Ikidluk standing before the masses. "I hereby issue this pronouncement that all who oppose my edicts and violate my laws are to be beheaded!"

Nena again added her commentary, "But by this time, Termaine had championed the great majority of the people to believe in themselves and to oppose his tyranny."

"What did Ikidluk do about that?" Ishim wondered.

The scene gave the answer. "I, Ikidluk, your ruler and God's representative here on Earth, hereby send my army to stifle this rebellion. I will not be opposed!"

Nena commented once again, "But the people believed in Termaine and in their just cause. Before Ikidluk knew it, many of his troops had turned on him and joined the people in their resistance. It wasn't long after that that the people banded together to drive Ikidluk from his castle. A great rallying cry was heard throughout the land that Termaine replace the tyrant as the first beloved King of the Great Mountain and all surrounding lands."

Nena paused to see if her audience was still attentive and when she saw that they were fully engrossed in her story, she continued to focus her thoughts so that they could observe the projection once again.

Termaine spoke to the enthusiastic throng from high upon the hillside, "I challenge you to step into your magnificence! I empower you to believe that anything is possible IF you believe it to be so! I invite you to make it so by believing in yourselves! I speak to you today of my great vision for you, your families, and your descendants. I envision that we can all join together to create a great subterranean city that will protect us all from the dangers of invasion or assault by Ikidluk, his followers, and any who might become emboldened to try to dominate us! This city will be a shining beacon of light where all can prosper and live in peace and abundance. I commit here and now to the challenge of leading you great people out from the tyrannical oppression of the tyrants who have treated you and your families as slaves, restricted your freedoms, and kept you subservient, in poverty and bondage! I know in my heart that you are capable of self-direction and self-government. My responsibility and the responsibility of those who ask to lead you is simply to empower you to realize your magnificent nature and capabilities and support you to step into your personal power to manifest your best lives, to realize your fullest, Creator-blessed potentials!"

Nena continued with her commentary, "During his reign, Termaine brought stability and peace to the land and implemented many social programs, including housing, health care, and transportation. He established sound political structures to share his ruling power with a Council he appointed who represented the diverse voices of the people. He championed many levels of public servants, always for the common good. His daughter, Ohma, my great-grandmother, became his trusted minister. She instituted the Great Halls of Learning and implemented many of the humanitarian and personal-development programs he began while expanding upon his vision for a just and empowered society that would accomplish great things for the good of all."

"So, tell us more about how the whole concept of the Septropolis had its origins," Plabius asked.

Nena went on, preferring to explain rather than focus on generating the scene, "Termaine and Ohma envisioned a great underground civilization to be constructed in the bedrock under the Great Mountain. This subterranean city was to become a model society where the arts and culture thrived while providing shelter, protection and the environment essential for the people to grow and prosper."

"In his 140th year, King Termaine was assassinated in a conspiracy formulated by the descendents of Ikidluk in a fierce battle for power. His grandson, Silvester, my grandfather, emerged victorious. In an effort to appease both those who opposed him and those who backed his enemies, he extended an olive branch to his adversaries, appointing many of them to positions on the Advisory Council and at various levels of authority. Although Silvester's intention was to embrace those with different perspectives, soon many began to plot against him and seek more personal power for themselves. Before long, Silvester lost his influence and the Great Council poisoned the minds of many of the people, allowing them to seize the real power and control."

"How soon people forget!" Plabius commented.

"Tell us about your parents," Ishim invited.

"My poor mother died in childbirth. My father, King Rey, Silvester's son, governed with fairness, love, generosity, and wisdom until I was 6 years old. At that time, there was a terrible accident, a misunderstanding really they say, and he was killed. I really don't want to get into all the details. The whole thing just upsets me too much. No one has discussed what happened with me since that day and besides, Ohma said I would learn the whole story one day when I was older. I really don't want to talk about that now. It is just too upsetting for me," Nena said, with tears streaming down both cheeks.

Sensing Nena's pain, Ishim did his best to change the subject. "So, Termaine and Ohma's vision for a great civilization based on empowerment and do-the-right-thing leadership was destroyed?"

"Many still held the vision but the treachery of the cunning Council members has been difficult to counter. They have been very persuasive in their arguments for greater control – of course for the benefit of the people they say! But we know better." Nena added. "I apologize but my strength wanes now."

"The insights we have learned from your story have been enlightening. Thank you for sharing this history with us!" Plabius gratefully acknowledged.

"Let us all rest now," added Ishim, "for there is much work ahead if we are to fulfill the prophesy of the scrolls."

Nena wanted so badly to know what Ishim meant,

but her body was still recovering from the fall and she knew that his explanation must wait, at least for now. As she closed her eyes, she wondered aloud, "Ohma always said that there are no accidents. Everything happens for a reason. It is always our responsibilities to watch for the signs and to decide upon what actions we must take. After all, the best way to predict the future is to invent it!"

Chapter 4

The Scrolls

Nena awakened to the smell of wild gourds and giant mushrooms roasting on the fire. Her long hours of rest were beginning to pay her with dividends of energy and renewed enthusiasm.

"Good day to you, Nena!" Plabius greeted her.

"You look so much better today," Ishim reassured.

"Thank you both, I do feel much better. My

arm sprain seems to be pretty well healed and I don't believe I'll need your handiwork any longer, Ishim," Nena smiled tossing aside her splint.

"That's wonderful news!" Ishim encouraged.

"I can't wait for you to tell me all about the scrolls you mentioned yesterday," Nena shouted, throwing up her arms and rising to her feet then clapping her hands twice.

"I can do better than that!" Plabius replied. "See for yourself."

He gently tossed two loosely wound parchment leaves to Nena.

She unfurled the first and read aloud...

IN TIMES SO DARK THAT THREATEN CREATION,

FOR THE EARTH TO SURVIVE AND AVOID ANNIHILATION,

THE NEED WILL ARISE FOR LEADERS SO BOLD,

WITH COURAGE TO THWART THE EVIL FORETOLD.

THE SECRETS TO SAVE OUR PLANET SO DEAR

WILL BE GIVEN TO THOSE WHO HAVE CONQUERED THEIR FEAR

AND QUEST TO DISCOVER THE MEANS TO REDEMPTION

FOR THE GOOD OF OTHERS WITHOUT AN EXCEPTION

TO SAVE THE WORLD FROM CERTAIN DESTRUCTION

AND DELIVER ITS PEOPLE FROM THEIR INTENDED PLIGHT

YOU MUST FREE THE ENSLAVED

AND EMPOWER THE HOPELESS

AND BRING THE SEVEN BLESSINGS TO LIGHT

Nena repeated the last sentence with emphasis, "and bring the seven blessings to light." She looked up at the concerned faces of her friends. "What do you think it means?"

"It sounds like a dire warning predicting the end of the world…unless we are successful in changing the path we are on as a people," Plabius suggested.

"Saving the world is NOT your responsibility Nena!" her companion reminded her.

"How do we know the scroll is speaking to us? This whole responsibility scares me!" Nena argued.

"There are no accidents, Nena. We found the scroll. You showed up. You discovered the plot to eliminate the Sumarians. We saved your life. We *are* Sumarians. You come from a long line of great leaders and aspire to leadership yourself. Is this all a big fat coincidence? I think not!"

"The Secrets to Save our Planet So Dear Will Be Given to Those Who Have Conquered Their Fear!" Ishim added. "What more of a golden invitation do you need to master your fear? Besides, my intuition tells me that we are the ones to make THE difference!"

"Ohma always said your intuition is never wrong. It is sourced in love and truth and you must learn to listen to it and act on it! She was always reminding me to listen to my intuition and trust it more. I have a tendency to give too much power to my fears instead" Nena shared.

"Now, remember that a little fear is a good thing! It keeps you from risking too much," Nena's companion warned.

"It's time to take action and act we will for time is precious," Plabius contributed. "Take a look at the second scroll."

Nena unfolded it slowly. "Why it's a map of all of the levels and the outer reaches of the Septropolis."

"Seven levels of a great city built above the site where they are hiding and torturing our people. Seven blessings we must discover according to the scroll. Another coincidence? I doubt it!" Plabius reasoned.

"I bet you are right," Nena nodded in agreement. "But how are we to discover these seven blessings?"

"If you look closely at the map, you can see where the first level of the Septropolis communicates with one of the vortices that was closed off by one of the explosions." Ishim pointed excitedly to the map. "I bet we can take the leeward path that communicates with that vortex and find our way to the outer reaches of the first level."

"So we can access the underground city undetected by entering its levels from the spaces created that surround it! Sounds like a plan," Nena agreed. "Even though I am afraid of what may await us, we have no choice but to act courageously in alignment with our commitments to your people and mine! I actually can't wait to get started!"

The companion shook her head back and forth and screeched.

Before Nena could finish her sentence, the three heard a rumbling high above in the ceiling of the cave.

"Quick, it appears they've found us!" Plabius exclaimed, gathering the scrolls and a pack of provisions.

The three scurried through an underground passage in the vortex floor and were off on their way through one of the many tunnels that traversed throughout the Inner World. Just moments later, they heard a thunderous explosion as their adversaries demolished the vortex chamber that had been their home for the past few days.

Chapter 5

The Septropolis

Holding some torches they put together, Plabius led the way, with Nena following closely behind and Ishim bringing up the rear. They jogged briskly for about three hours. Where the passage opened up and allowed enough room for it, Plabius held Nena's hand on one side and Ishim flanked her on the other so that the two could fly through the air with Nena in the middle.

"Flying has its advantages! It's also a good thing we are all in great physical condition!" Nena observed. "It appears that these tunnels go on forever."

"I have navigated my way through these passages on many an occasion," Plabius added. "We should be near the vortex opening that the map shows to communicate with the outer reaches of the first level of the Septropolis."

"The map shows a narrow passage leading to what's referred to as the Vision Chamber," Ishim observed.

The three forged their way ahead, climbing over boulders and other debris that was strewn along the passage from the renegade Council members' efforts to destroy the vortex channels.

"Look!" Ishim whispered, pointing to a black door with rusty hinges at the top of an outcropping of rock just ahead of the group. "Wait here, while I make sure the coast is clear."

As Plabius and Nena waited below in the passage, Ishim flew up onto the rock with torch in hand and approached the door. He turned the door handle slowly and to his surprise, it creaked open. Glancing inside to the left and right, he saw that the chamber was empty. He thrust the torch into the ground outside the chamber and as he entered the room, he quietly closed the door behind him. In an instant, an image appeared on the massive 360-degree screen that surrounded him. He realized he was in some sort of a theater or projection room. A narrow passageway wide enough for only one person to pass through terminated in a small round spot in the middle of the room, just large enough to stand upon. Ishim cautiously edged forward step by step. As he reached the small stage in the room's center, a railing rose up around him, allowing him to comfortably lean upon it.

"Welcome, Ishim!" a voice greeted him.

"How do you know my name?" he replied in a cautious whisper.

"You are in the Vision Chamber," came the immediate reply.

As he looked all around him, he beheld a scene all too familiar. He was watching the story of his life!

The scene progressed from when Ishim was a young child. Before his eyes, he once again experienced the pain of bullies making fun of him because he was different. The Earth Change had created several new races but only the Sumarians possessed wings.

"Bird boy, bird boy, bird boy!" they chanted.

Ishim felt the familiar shame and rage run up his back, causing the hairs on his neck to stand at attention. His face flushed with embarrassment.

"How I hate these darn wings!" he muttered.

Ishim closed his eyes momentarily to regain his composure as he recalled his troubled early years before meeting his good friend Plabius. He opened his eyes to see the scene shift to one where those same children were joyfully playing side by side with him and his Sumarian friends. He watched as his projected counterpart on the screen sat in a circle with dignitaries from many races. He realized that he was witnessing his dream of bringing peace and harmony to all the races.

The scene shifted once again and he saw himself

seated in the Council Chamber along with many other leaders committed to creating a new paradigm for harmonious interaction among all people.

As he continued to watch for what seemed like an instant to him, and an eternity to his concerned friends waiting in the passage outside the door, he realized that he was experiencing the projection of his vision for his life. He was at the same time inspired by what he saw and compelled to bring it into manifestation in the real world.

How and why was *his* vision instead of someone more important than him being displayed in the chamber? This was the question he pondered as he walked back out of the chamber through the black door with the rusty hinges to greet his friends.

"You're all right!" Nena exclaimed as Ishim emerged through the door.

"We were certainly getting worried!" Plabius added. "In fact, I was just about ready to come in and save you!" he said smiling.

"There's no one in there. It's perfectly safe. This

is the only door that accesses the chamber. And, you're not going to believe what's playing in this theater!"

"What?" Plabius wondered aloud.

"It's the story of my life as I would wish it to unfold, in vivid and explicit detail!" Ishim revealed with a tear in his eye, obviously moved by the experience.

"Can we watch it?" Nena asked eagerly.

"Yes, you both can. But I suggest that you go in first, while Plabius and I keep watch out here. If any of our enemies should come along, it's better that we both be here to deal with them, instead of only one of us."

"Very well, I'll wait here with Ishim while you go and watch his story," Plabius encouraged, motioning to Nena to scoot along.

Ishim and Plabius gave Nena a boost up to the knoll the door sat upon. She opened it cautiously and seeing that the chamber was safe and just as Ishim had described it, she ventured in. She proceeded down the same small path reaching the floor in the middle of the room.

"Welcome, Nena!" came the booming greeting.

Nena froze, not knowing if she was supposed to respond or not.

"It's a trap! Just as I suspected," snapped the companion.

As Nena stood motionless, awaiting what would happen next, the light of the projector filled the circular room. Nena turned left, then right, then behind her, grasping onto the railing.

"Why Ishim was wrong! His story isn't featured here. Mine is!" she muttered to her companion. "I understand now. This room highlights the vision of its occupant, and right now, that happens to be me!"

Nena watched the screen that surrounded her as the story began with her birth. She observed the tremendous joy in her mother's eyes as she beheld her precious little girl. She again felt the pain of separation as she watched her mother die of internal bleeding as a result of complications with her birth.

The scene shifted to the castle on the hill where Nena lived with her father until his untimely death when she was 6 years old. Nena's heart swelled as she saw her father, King Rey, peer out his dressing room window. Nena continued to watch the vision screen. She watched the 6-year-old Nena cry out in anguish, yelling hysterically. She realized she had just witnessed her beloved father's death.

A moment later the screen was black.

What seemed like an eternity passed as Nena sat in the darkness.

"We're out of here!" Nena's companion shouted.

"I want to see this!" she countered. "I have a right to remember what happened! What kind of conspiracy is this?"

But the room remained dark for a few minutes longer.

Soon, a new scene resumed as though there were a break in the film.

"I will raise you as my own daughter!" comforted the loving and gentle soul she recognized as her great-grandmother, the kindred spirit she would call Ohma, a name that soon came to mean love and inspiration to her as it did to so many others. "Although you are fatherless and your poor mother left this world so that you might enter it, I shall be your loving guardian, your friend, and your family for the rest of my days."

Nena felt a tear well up in her eye as she realized how much she loved her Ohma. "I hope and pray that she is safe right now," she whispered.

"She's probably in prison or dead by now!" the companion said. Nena ignored her.

For several seconds, Nena stood in the dark room, composing herself. When she had done so sufficiently, the projection continued.

Nena watched as the young girl grew into a young woman, bathed in the unending love and continual empowerment of her great-grandmother.

"I owe who I am all to you, Ohma," she whispered in gratitude.

Nena saw the image of herself growing into her twenties, stepping into leadership to save her planet and its people. She watched as she rallied the people with her call for 'do the right thing' leadership. She was humbled by scene after scene of people who respected her leadership and were empowered to live lives of magnificence thanks to her inspiration. She felt an overwhelming sense of love and trust for all people consume her. She saw her friends, Plabius and Ishim, work tirelessly with her as they all championed the just causes that brought hope, peace, happiness, and abundance to the world's people.

"I had better move along and give Plabius some time to experience his vision," Nena thought to herself.

And so, she returned to find her friends patiently awaiting her return. Plabius took his place in the Vision Chamber's center and he too witnessed his grandest dreams unfold before his eyes. With a tear in his eye, he returned to his friends.

As he closed the door, a banner unfurled. It read...

"A VISION THAT PASSIONATELY INSPIRES YOU TO BE YOUR BEST, TO CONTRIBUTE YOUR GIFTS TO OTHERS, AND MAKES YOUR LIFE HAPPY AND FULFILLED IS A TRUE BLESSING."

Plabius, and Ishim collected the banner and Nena tucked it safely into her knapsack.

Chapter 6

Ohma's Plight

The three friends, richer from experiencing their first blessing, now prepared to continue their quest to discover the remaining blessings, free the Sumarians, and return 'do the right thing' leadership to the world.

"One thing I am unclear about is this," Ishim wondered. "Is what we saw *definitely* going to happen or is it only *possibly* going to happen?"

"I suppose that is really up to us!" Nena responded. "To the extent that we see our visions as inevitable, we will be empowered to manifest them."

"But what if our enemies have visions that are in direct opposition to our visions?" Plabius interjected.

"Whose vision becomes reality then?"

"It would have to be the person with the stronger vision," Nena reasoned. "I believe that what we experienced was an empowering possibility that we can each pursue with passion."

"So, you are saying that a powerful vision is a place to start from, rather than a guaranteed outcome?" Plabius questioned.

"Exactly!" Nena confirmed. "It is a dream that sets the tone for our actions to align with. It is a true blessing because it gives our lives direction and purpose."

"So, powerful visions can't be just about the person with the vision?" Ishim queried.

"Right! To be powerful, they must include other people. What kind of vision is just about you? A selfish and shallow one, I say," Plabius added. "And one that only motivates you, but others couldn't care less about."

Nena interrupted, "That's the kind of visions that the renegade Council members have. Selfish, self-serving, greedy, and heartless ones!"

"It's no wonder why the world is in such a shambles with leaders with those kinds of visions running the show!" Nena's companion shook her head in disgust.

"I just feel blessed to share such an empowering vision for the betterment of the world with two great friends like you!" Plabius blurted out, a bit embarrassed by his sudden show of emotion.

"One thing that the Vision Chamber reminded me of is Ohma," Nena added somberly. "I sure hope she is all right. I'd guess that the evil Council members might take out their revenge on her if they think I might cause trouble for them."

"This map shows the location of the Septropolis' holding cells on the West Wing of Level 2. If your Ohma is in trouble, I bet that's where she'll be," Plabius reasoned.

"Let's head there now to check it out," Nena asserted.

"Fine with me," Plabius responded.

"Me too," Ishim added.

And so the three friends followed the map's route

that pointed the way to the holding cells. They had to climb down a steep incline in the cavity that surrounded the Septropolis' outer wall. With the last Earth Change, many such cavities, tunnels, cracks, caves, and chasms opened up on all sides of the underground city that had been hewn from solid stone. It was through one such chasm that Nena, Plabius, and Ishim now climbed (and flew), downward toward the structure that had been built outside the walls of the city. The misguided Council members envisioned its original purpose to be a place to house criminals, the insane, and other "undesirables" who would embarrass the better members of their society.

"The map shows two guard stations on either side of the entrance to the holding cells," Ishim observed. "I'll try to distract the guard here. When I do, you and Nena climb through this vent in the floor to see what you can find out."

"That's far too dangerous a plan," the companion commented.

"Please do be careful, Ishim!" Nena pleaded.

"Don't you worry about me, my friend. I may be

a misfit but I'm faster than any guard can hope to be," he reassured her.

Nena and Plabius quietly followed the passage leading to the air vent that surfaced just next to the West Wing guard post. From their perch beneath the vent, Plabius could see the guard's weapon leaning against the wall.

"Hey, you, I'm looking for my uncle," Ishim yelled, capturing the guard's attention.

"You're not supposed to be in here!" the guard yelled back, springing from his seat in pursuit of Ishim. As he gained ground on Ishim, he continued, "You're one of those vermin! I'll get you and put you in the hole where you belong!"

Ishim took to flight with the guard in hot pursuit.

"Quick, now's our chance!" beckoned Plabius to Nena.

With a firm push, Plabius loosened the grate and the two climbed out into the hallway where a dozen cells lined each side of the West Wing corridor. The clamor of the prisoners who now sensed a disturbance grew louder.

Nena began to look into the small windows lined with bars on one side of the hallway while Plabius did likewise on the other side.

"Most of these prisoners look like they've been tortured!" Plabius commented in disgust.

"Ohma!" Nena cried out, as she peered into a cell in the middle of the row. "I've found you!"

"Nena, I knew you would! But it's far too dangerous for you to be here, my child," she continued.

"Plabius, help me," Nena commanded.

Plabius placed his hands on the windows' bars and in a few seconds pulled them apart as if they were made of clay, not iron.

"Another of your gifts?" Nena smiled.

"The Earth Change brought us many," he concurred.

Plabius reached in and performed the same feat on the iron lock that bolted the door shut. Ohma was chained to the far wall by her wrists and ankles. In a matter of seconds, Plabius had melted her shackles and the prisoner was free.

"Come, we must hurry!" Plabius pleaded.

Ohma was still stiff from being chained for days and the bruises on her arms and back told of the multiple beatings she had suffered as her captors tried to learn the whereabouts of her great-granddaughter.

Nena supported Ohma on one side and Plabius on the other. Soon they had all made their way back through the floor grate and into the passage. Plabius secured the grate in place as they exited the hall.

"Are you okay, Ohma?" Nena asked, tears running down her cheek as she saw close up what her Ohma had been put through because of *her* discovery.

"I'll be fine, my dear," Ohma reassured her. "It's nothing that a few days of rest and care won't cure."

"I'm sorry, with all the commotion, I forgot to introduce you. Ohma, this is my friend Plabius. He saved my life just as I was about to be mauled by the evil Council members' hounds. Plabius, meet my great-grandmother, Ohma."

"It's a great honor to meet you, madam," Plabius

nodded respectfully. "I am well acquainted with your illustrious history of leadership and contribution to the world. Nena has told me all about you."

"The honor is mine, my son," Ohma countered. "Thank you so much for saving my Nena and for rescuing me!"

"You are very welcome. It is my privilege," Plabius added.

"I see you are Sumarian. My captors were relentless in grilling me about the locations of your people," Ohma offered. "Of course, although I had heard rumors of your winged race, I was just beginning to put the pieces together. The Council had operated covertly up until the last few days. They seem to have banded together now with a common mission."

"Yes, hatred and annihilation!" Nena interrupted.

"I hope they all die a painful death!" Nena's companion added.

"Now, my dear, consider your words and desires carefully. Responding to hatred with hatred and to evil with evil is not the answer," Ohma counseled.

"They have killed and tortured so many of our people," Plabius spoke up. "And they have done the same to those among your people who have opposed them!"

"I am certainly not condoning their actions, my dears. I do not approve of their prejudicial views or of their horrific tactics. All I am saying is that it serves us not to lower ourselves to their level by letting our hearts be consumed with hatred and vengeance."

"How should we look upon this whole situation then, madam?" Plabius queried, anxious to learn from this wise and kind leader.

"We all act from pictures we hold in our minds about how we see ourselves, how we see others, and how we see the world. Rather than react to the words, deeds, and aggressions of others, it is wiser to assume that they do the best they know how, based upon how they perceive what is required for them to survive and thrive in what they see to be a stressful and difficult world."

"But their actions make me want to kill them!"

Plabius contested angrily.

"So you are at the affect of what they do, dear?" Ohma asked.

"I suppose I am," Plabius responded.

"And I assert that being reactive does not support who you are, who any of us are. Rather, ask yourself the question, 'What must it be like in their world for them to see things as they do? For them to be filled with such hatred? For them to want to annihilate your people? For them to want to develop weapons of such destructive power that they now threaten even their own very survival?"

"They must be very afraid and see our people as a threat to their very survival," Plabius offered, now understanding Ohma's point.

"They must see the world as a place of scarcity, suffering, and competition for resources that others want to take from them," Nena added.

"Very good! And they must think that the only way to avoid being dominated by others is to dominate them first!" Ohma offered.

"So, are we not to oppose them just because they view things in their own way based upon how they perceive what they must do?" Plabius asked.

"I did not say that. You have every right to defend yourselves and to protect your people. It just does not serve you to allow them to trigger your fears, to make you so angry that you forget who you are and what is most important to you. Because if you do, you sacrifice who you really are, you dishonor your own goodness and forfeit your right to honor your most important values."

"So let us then be a force for good in the world and look for ways to help them see the error in their thinking. For I now see that we will not persuade them by being like them. We will only have a chance to enlighten them if we are true to our principles and act from the perspective of what supports us while understanding the reasons behind why they act as they do," Nena said.

As they turned a corner in the passage way, they could see Ishim approaching them from the opposite direction with a broad smile on his face. He was carrying a flag he had found that said,

"EMPATHY FOR WHAT IT IS LIKE IN YOUR NEIGHBOR'S WORLD IS A TRUE BLESSING."

Plabius and Nena ran up to and embraced Ishim.

"We were so worried that the guard caught you!" Nena cried as she squeezed him tightly.

"I told you not to worry. I knew he'd be no match for my speed," Ishim reassured them smiling, quite proud of his accomplishment. "Besides, he couldn't fly!"

"Ohma, it is my honor to introduce you to our brave friend, Ishim. Ishim also helped save my life and nursed me back to health. Not to mention that it was his idea to distract the guard so that Plabius and I could rescue you."

"Thank you from the bottom of my heart, brave and honorable sir!" Ohma congratulated with a tear in her eye. "Without your courage and selflessness, I would still be chained to my cell, awaiting my next beating."

"It is my pleasure to contribute to one who has

contributed to so many," Ishim smiled, bowing politely.

The three filled Ishim in about their discussion that brought to light the mindset of their misguided adversaries.

"Now the flag I found makes perfect sense," Ishim offered. "I had an idea that I'd be learning more about its important message."

"What does the map tell us about our next destination?" Nena asked.

"Where did you get the map?" Ohma questioned.

"I apologize, Ohma. We forgot to tell you about the scroll and the map that Plabius and Ishim found in the cave near the vortex passage where I recovered from my fall."

Plabius pulled out the first scroll and presented it to Ohma.

Holding it close to her face, Ohma read it intently.

IN TIMES SO DARK THAT THREATEN CREATION,

FOR THE EARTH TO SURVIVE AND AVOID ANNIHILATION,

THE NEED WILL ARISE FOR LEADERS SO BOLD,

WITH COURAGE TO THWART THE EVIL FORETOLD.

THE SECRETS TO SAVE OUR PLANET SO DEAR

WILL BE GIVEN TO THOSE WHO HAVE CONQUERED THEIR FEAR

AND QUEST TO DISCOVER THE MEANS TO REDEMPTION

FOR THE GOOD OF OTHERS WITHOUT AN EXCEPTION

TO SAVE THE WORLD FROM CERTAIN DESTRUCTION

AND DELIVER ITS PEOPLE FROM THEIR INTENDED PLIGHT

YOU MUST FREE THE ENSLAVED

AND EMPOWER THE HOPELESS

AND BRING THE SEVEN BLESSINGS TO LIGHT

"I now understand," Ohma nodded solemnly. "I have opposed the testing the Council leaders had been prosing for some years. I can see now that the damage done to our Earth beyond the boundaries of the Septropolis has been significant."

"They are torturing and killing our Sumarian people

at a site that is said to be beneath the Septropolis' seventh level," Plabius shared.

"And so, our mission is clear, according to the scroll. We must free the innocent prisoners and discover the seven blessings that will give our planet a fighting chance to avoid the annihilation that has been foretold." Ohma continued.

"You have the gift of prophesy, Ohma," Nena reminded. "Can you look into the future and tell us if our efforts will prevail?"

"I can tell you what will happen if you do not try your very best," Ohma replied. "Without our efforts, the Sumarian people will be annihilated and many of our friends and countrymen who are political prisoners will be tortured and murdered. Beyond that, it does not serve you to know more. Now, may I see the map you have, please?"

Ishim handed Ohma the map.

"I see that Level 3 of the Septropolis is adjacent to the Sacred Pool that empties into the Great River that runs from the World Above to continue its course along much of the Inner World. The map suggests that our path should coincide with the Pool at Level 3," Ohma observed, pointing to the location on the map so all could see.

"I've heard tales of the Sacred Pool's powers from many of our people," Plabius shared.

"What kinds of powers?" Nena asked.

"I'm not sure. All I know is that those who experienced them were forever impacted for the better," Plabius added. "Many said their experience was life changing."

The group continued onward for the rest of the day. They had to make frequent stops to allow Ohma to rest, even though they carried her during much of the journey on a stretcher they crafted from materials they found along the way.

"Let's set up camp here for the night," suggested Plabius.

And so the group slept soundly with a better appreciation for what it is like in the world of others while awaiting their next adventure.

Chapter 7

The Sacred Pool

The good night's sleep Ohma finally got after several days chained to the prison wall did her a world of good. Nena rested soundly too, knowing that Ohma was safe by her side. Plabius and Ishim took turns standing watch, but thankfully, the night was uneventful.

"You both look wonderful this morning!" Plabius congratulated Nena and Ohma. "We've got quite a bit of ground to cover today if we are to reach the Sacred Pool before nightfall."

Ishim handed out the morning's breakfast provisions to all, taking great care not to waste any of the precious provisions he had stashed away in his knapsack before their speedy exit from the vortex cave two days before.

"Are we ready?" Plabius prodded.

"Ready, willing, and hopefully able," Ohma shot back.

"Great! Let's go then," Ishim encouraged.

"What does the map have to say about the Sacred Pool?" Nena asked.

Ishim pulled out the map and read the caption, "The Sacred Pool is a mystical underground lake known for its healing powers."

"What else does it say?" Plabius queried.

"That's all it says. I suppose we will have to discover for ourselves what those healing powers are all about."

Encouraged by Ishim's brief description, the group made good progress along their path. Ohma was able to keep pace on her own for the most part, with Plabius and Ishim carrying her between them whenever the terrain allowed them to take flight and gain ground. Nena had little difficulty keeping up, due to her great physical conditioning.

As the group began their descent down a steep hill, Ishim let out a shout of jubilation, "Look! Down there, can you see the shimmering green waters? That must be the Sacred Pool."

"Plabius and I will wait here for now. Nena, will you go ahead and make sure the coast is clear so that we may descend? Once you give us the sign, we will help Ohma get down this steep and potentially dangerous grade."

"You go! It's too dangerous for Nena," the companion interjected.

Ignoring her chatter, Nena volunteered, "Sure thing! I'll be happy to check it out."

"Please be careful, Nena. We've been fortunate so far but surely search parties alerted by the guard at the Detention Center must be on the lookout for us," Ohma implored.

Nena cautiously made her way down the steep and rugged incline and in about 30 minutes she found herself at the water's edge.

"Why, this is the most beautiful lake I've ever seen!" she whispered to her companion, in awe.

Nena could see the entire shoreline of the tiny lake from where she stood. Its sparkling green color reflected the trees lining its shore. After looking in every direction, she turned around and could see her friends perched high on the cliff terrace, a mile or so away.

Waving her arms to signal, she yelled "It's safe! Come on down!"

As she waited for the three to make their descent, hot and dirty from her journey, Nena dived into the refreshing emerald green waters of the lake. As she surfaced, shaking the water out of her ears and brushing the hair from her face, she was astounded by the three-dimensional sight she suddenly beheld.

A painful sense of longing returned to her heart and she felt that familiar upset jab at her stomach. High on the cliff reflected in the green waters before her stood the castle she recalled as her regal home in her earliest days. Her jaw dropped as she now caught sight of her beloved father high up in the window of the castle. The scene slowly returned to her memory in bits and pieces. King Rey was obviously startled by something he saw from his high perch in the castle tower on the cliff that overlooked the ocean.

Nena watched as her father, dressed in the old robe he had worn only before her and Ohma in his private chambers, now ran out in front of the castle lawn, jumping up and down, flailing his arms and shouting something that neither Nena nor the people whose attention he was trying to attract could hear.

Seconds later she watched as her beloved father carried her young body half asleep from her bedroom chamber, down the castle's grand staircase and out the door. King Rey had placed her safely inside a fenced area far from the castle entrance.

Nena experienced again the same painful scene she had blocked from her memory for so long.

"You don't have to watch this!" her companion offered.

"I want to!" Nena mumbled.

She watched in amazement as her father tore down the royal flags that hung from two poles flanking the main entrance door to the castle. He took the flags and lit them with the flame that burned from the adjacent lantern. The king next ran inside the castle and within a few minutes, the entire structure was ablaze.

King Rey, still clothed only in his old robe, then ran back out the door onto the lawn that separated his beloved castle and the sea far below the cliff upon which it stood.

Nena watched in horror and disbelief as one of the royal guards, who had observed the burning of the castle, slowly drew his bow and took aim. Thinking it to be the work of a crazy arsonist, the guard launched an arrow that hit its target, piercing the heart of her beloved father.

Raging anger welled up once again in her heart. Both Nena and her companion shouted hysterically together, "How could he? How could he!"

Nena closed her eyes, not knowing if she could continue to relive any more of the horrific spectacle. Reminding herself of her need to see the rest of the scene, she willed her eyes open once again.

Nena could now see a grand celebration taking place on the beach, far below the castle perched on the cliff above. She watched as the group's attention turned from their festivities to the castle, now fully engulfed in flames high up on the hill. Nena watched as nearly half of the partiers made their difficult way up the steep hill in an effort to lend assistance in hope of saving the castle from total destruction.

Nena was shocked to observe the rest of the group apparently uninterested in lending a hand. Many could be seen to dismiss the need to help save the castle. She heard one say, "It's not my castle. Why should I rush up that steep hill?" Another spoke, "The king is wealthy and can easily afford to build a new castle!" And so, others spoke likewise, returning to their festivities with an apparent indifferent air.

"Why, they just can't be bothered!" Nena's companion murmured to her in disgust.

Nena watched as the first group worked feverishly to save the castle.

Her perspective now shifted to show the view from the top of the cliff toward the beach. Nena realized in an instant that she now shared the same view her father had in the last minutes of his life, a view that eluded her as the young child trapped safely behind the fence.

"Oh my!" she exclaimed in disbelief. The entire scene finally made sense to her!

Nena could see a great tidal wave far off at sea, but quickly approaching the shore. The revelers on the beach lacked this perspective and continued eating, drinking, and dancing.

"No wonder why my father acted as he did!" she whispered.

Nena heard a sound and turned from the scene back toward her own shore line. There she saw Ohma, Plabius, and Ishim. They all had been watching the scene unfold before them, just as Nena had.

"I foresaw this day long ago and knew it best that you experience the entire story from the Sacred Pool!" Ohma cried to Nena from shore. "Your blessed father could see the tidal wave approaching from his window high above on the cliff. He tried to yell and warn the people on shore, but they could not hear him."

"Who were they? The ones on shore, I mean." Nena asked.

"They were a party of ambassadors from many other nations that your father, King Rey, had invited to the castle grounds to share their ideas, talk of peace and commerce, and other important matters. The king had just begun to change his clothes in preparation to join them on the beach when he spotted the giant wave approaching the shore. Because the group on the beach could not hear his warning cries, he set his own home on fire in an effort to catch their attention so they might be saved!"

"But why did only some respond?" Nena wondered aloud.

"It is certainly ironic. The ones who cared more about offering their help to another in his time of need climbed the steep hill and their lives were spared. Those who chose their own selfish pleasures and returned to their food, drink, and revelries over the chance to help were obliged to meet their end," Ohma explained.

"But how could that evil man shoot my father?" Nena sobbed.

"We will NEVER forgive him until the day we die! We wish he could experience the very same pain he has caused us to bear!" her companion added.

Ohma went on, "The guard who shot his arrow did so with the best intentions. He thought someone had surely lost his mind and was setting the castle on fire and trying to kill the king. He did not recognize your father in his robe and had no idea it was actually his beloved king, the very person he was trying to protect!"

"How could he have been so stupid! He shoots first and asks questions later? That is unforgiveable!" Nena's companion interjected.

"No wonder why I trust no one except for you," Nena added.

"I see that you will need to grow in empathy and wisdom, and that time will come, my dear," consoled her loving great-grandmother.

"So my father sacrificed his home and castle and ended up giving his own life so that many others could be saved! It makes me love him even more when I think about it," Nena wept.

"And those who sacrificed their merriment in the service of another were saved, while the selfish and greedy perished," Ohma concluded.

The group heard the flapping sound coming from a few yards up on the shore. As they turned to see where the noise came from, they observed a flag flying proudly from a tree limb gracing the shore. It read:

"UNSELFISH CONTRIBUTION TO THE LIVES OF OTHERS

IS A SACRED BLESSING."

Chapter 8

The Gifts of the Grotto

Painful as it was to experience, the scene at the Sacred Pool finally allowed Nena to achieve some measure of completion regarding her father's death.

"I am humbled that my father's love for others was so great that he would destroy his beloved home and end up giving his very life in contribution to others. He was truly a great man! He was truly a great man!" Nena repeated over and over to the others.

"He *was* truly a great man," Plabius added.

"An inspiration to me," Ishim chimed in.

"Sleep now, my dear child, and know that although your father now lives in shadow, his spirit and love are with you always," Ohma consoled.

Nena closed her eyes, gave thanks for the comfort of learning about her father's sacrifice, and fell soundly asleep, her body and mind thoroughly exhausted as a result of the day's events.

Early the next morning, Plabius heard a noise, sprang to his feet and abruptly awakened his sleeping friends. "Hurry, hurry, Nena, Ohma, Ishim. We must leave right away!"

Nena looked up upon the ledge that the group had climbed down from the previous day. A search party consisting of two soldiers and a dog had followed their trail and were now rapidly making their way down the hillside.

"Quickly!" Ishim yelled, pointing to a small boat that was tied to a tree just a few dozen yards from their camp.

Plabius grabbed Ohma and Ishim took Nena by the arm. Within a few seconds the men had flown over to the craft and placed Nena and Ohma inside the small vessel before shoving off.

As their row boat floated off down the lake toward the Hillcay River, the soldiers and their dog arrived at the site where they had just been moments ago on shore. Both men reached into their quivers and fired arrows at the group, but they were now far enough away so that the arrows fell harmlessly into the boat's wake.

"Now what?" wondered Nena aloud.

"What does the map show?" Plabius asked, gesturing to Ishim.

Ishim pulled out the map. The trail outlined on it showed that for the group to reach their intended destination on Level 4 of the Septropolis, they would need to proceed several miles down the Hillcay River, arriving at a small beach where a narrow path led to the destination marked by a big red X on the map.

"I'm getting pretty tired of this!" Ishim moaned with a big scowl on his face.

"Tired of what?" Nena asked.

"Tired of being different. Tired of people wanting

to kill me! Tired of being a freak! Tired of these wings. Tired of not having a family that cares about me. I'm just sick and tired of EVERYTHING!" Ishim shouted.

"I sense you may gain a different perspective shortly," Ohma smiled in a knowing way that only one with the gift of perceiving the future can.

"Look!" Plabius cried. "The river runs through a dark grotto up ahead. Prepare yourselves for the unexpected!"

The small craft was now caught up in the river's current, heading straight for the grotto.

"Duck down now!" Plabius ordered.

The others complied and soon all four were lying on their backs looking up at the ceiling of the grotto.

Ishim looked up in awe. He rubbed his eyes as if questioning their accuracy. Before him on the ceiling was a specter he readily recognized as himself. He was surrounded by several other apparitions he soon determined to be his spirit guides.

"Let's see what you most need to learn in this

lifetime," said a familiar voice Ishim had heard before in times when he most needed guidance.

The guide went on to present Ishim with a beautifully wrapped present tied up with a lovely yellow bow. "Humility. Yes, that will take care of that arrogant streak." He continued to present Ishim with a second red gift. "Compassion. Yes, you will need lessons in suffering. It's not all about you, Ishim, after all!" And then, here's a third present, "Patience, because you must learn to love the process and know that all good things will come to you eventually."

Ishim watched as a second spirit approached his ghostly counterpart.

While handing him a box wrapped in a blue bow, she spoke. "Accomplishment. That will build your self-esteem." Then a black box labeled Problems. "You'll need to overcome your share of challenges, of course." And lastly, a red box marked Courage. "This should support you to overcome whatever obstacles you encounter."

Ishim stared at the grotto scene, fascinated at the

planning that had obviously preceded his birth. A third ghost approached him with a green present. “Love, this will not come easy for you, but fear not, my friend, it *will* come!” The spirit continued. “Here, Ishim, is the gift of commitment. You will need this when the going gets tough.” The third spirit placed his arm around Ishim and patted him on the back. “This gift will both teach you empathy and give you an advantage over those who wish to thwart your noble goals. Here, Ishim, are your wings!” handing this last gift over.

Ishim bowed his head from his supine position in the boat, tears of joy rolling down his cheeks. “How could I have not realized how truly blessed I am! I now see that I have everything I need and more! I am so grateful! Even my wings are a blessing. And I was the last to realize this.”

As their small boat drifted with the river current exiting the grotto, Ishim could see from the expressions on his friends’ faces that they too had experienced a full revelation of what each one possessed as their special, unique, and awesome gifts.

“That had to be the most empowering experience I’ve ever had!” Nena declared. “I am humbled and so very grateful.”

“What are your gifts, Nena?” Ohma asked.

“Too many too count! But inspiration, contribution, wisdom, and love were the top four I’d say,” Nena smiled.

“That makes sense. Those are among my top values as well!” Ohma shared. “What about you, Plabius?”

“Joy, caring, friendship, and courage, to name just a few,” Plabius responded. “How about you, Ishim?”

“I am so very blessed! Even my wings are a gift that provides me with athleticism, uniqueness, compassion, humility, and empathy! I’d tell you about more of my many gifts, but I don’t want to brag too much!” Ishim laughed, causing the others to burst into laughter along with him.

As the boat rounded the river bend, Plabius spotted a flag on the shore in the distance. “I bet that is the spot marked by the X on the map.”

The craft soon floated ashore. Ishim pulled the flag from the ground marking the entrance to the fourth level of the Septropolis. Reading its message aloud, Ishim said…

"EVERY PERSON IS BLESSED WITH A MULTITUDE OF UNIQUE GIFTS. THE CHOICE IS YOURS TO BE GRATEFUL AND MAKE THE MOST OF THESE BLESSINGS OR FOCUS INSTEAD ON ALL YOUR PETTY CONCERNS."

Chapter 9

The Rocky Gorge

The group made their camp on shore that evening. Although they had experienced a remarkable day and needed their rest, no one could fall asleep so they decided to enjoy each other's company for a while and discuss their insights.

"I can't believe how differently I see things now than I did earlier today!" Ishim began the conversation.

"I have to admit that I was feeling sorry for myself. You know, poor, poor pitiful me!" he laughed.

"It's so easy to lose sight of the many things we all have to be grateful about," Ohma agreed. "I know that there have been too many times in my long life when I doubted my ability to thrive and access the love and abundance we see others tapping into. Too often, I've thought 'Hey! What about me? Where's my share?"

"I suppose its just human nature to react to our fears of scarcity and our expectations of failure, hurt, and disappointment," Plabius chipped in.

"We see ourselves in competition with others for love and attention, as well as for the world's resources, rather than realizing that there is more than enough good to go around," Ohma added.

"So, if I understand you correctly, Ohma, you are saying that whenever we forget that we are magnificent beings and that there is plenty of wealth, happiness, fun, and fulfillment to go around, we might feel the need to protect ourselves from what we perceive to be a dangerous world?" Nena wondered.

"Exactly right, my darling girl," Ohma affirmed. "Just look at every word out of your companion's mouth as suspect. That little negative chatterer is always on edge trying to warn you of some manufactured threat! Recognizing that her advice most often does not serve you is the first step. After that, it's your job to come up with an interpretation that supports your relationships, happiness, and personal power. We also tend to forget that others operate from the same lacking self-confidence, scarcity of gratitude, and deficient self-love that we often do."

"So, that's why the Council members are threatened by the Sumarians!" Ishim asserted. "It's really about them, not about us. If they felt like they had what it takes to not only survive, but thrive in this world, they wouldn't fear losing control to a people who are just different than they are."

Plabius added, "Yes, Ishim, they fear that we will dominate them and compete for what they see as scarce resources. When we stop to realize that everyone suffers from the same self-doubt and fear of being dominated or cheated out of getting their fair share of love, wealth, fun, and security, we can break the vicious cycle of endless competition and that constant striving for domination!"

"Why can't everyone see that cooperation and communication are more effective in producing harmony than competition and a focus on self-interest based on fear?" Nena shook her head.

"We can intentionally choose to trust that others are doing the best they know how to do based on how they see the world," Ohma replied. "We can commit to doing our best to support them to see another way, to view a situation other than from fear, hatred, or scarcity. Remember, my children, even when others act poorly, we still can retain control over our response to any situation. We can give up our right to be invalidated. We can exit the reactive cycle of conflict by choosing understanding, compassion, and love...always."

"What that means to me, Ohma, is that we can

decide to welcome challenges and see problems such as this one with the Council members as opportunities for our growth and development," Nena added.

"I am so proud of you all!" Ohma congratulated.

Nena's companion looked at her like she had two heads.

Ohma continued, "Be grateful for the challenges you encounter as you go about your day. Each one contains gifts awaiting our discovery!"

With the peace that the group felt in their hearts from the lessons of the day, they closed their eyes and drifted off to sleep.

Ishim was the first to arise the next morning. He quietly slipped off to the river's edge and soon he had caught enough big, fat juicy fish to surprise his friends with a wonderful breakfast feast.

The four eat heartily, appreciating the change from

what were now week-old seed cakes and grain loaves.

"Today, we will need to journey down a steep stony pass hewn from solid rock from centuries of erosion caused by the great waterfall," Ishim instructed, pointing to the map that showed the Hillcay River's termination at the falls that marked the Great Rocky Gorge. "This pass will lead us to Level 5 of the Septropolis."

"What are these markings?" Plabius asked, putting his finger upon three red triangles along the trail outlined on the map.

"Those are danger warnings. It looks like the trail is both steep and treacherous in those locations," Ishim explained. "Nena, I suggest you lead the way during the next leg of the journey so that Plabius and I can best support Ohma to descend the rocks, which will likely be slippery in spots from the fall's mist."

"If this trail is as dangerous as you seem to think it will be, why wouldn't you lead the way, Ishim?" Nena's companion asked.

"Plabius and I can assist Ohma just as well

as you can," Nena added, obviously heeding her companion's advice.

"Very well, Nena, if that is what you prefer," Ishim agreed, sensing the mistrust in Nena's voice. "I did not suggest you lead to put you at risk. I just thought that I could be of greater service with Plabius and Ohma."

Ishim could tell from Nena's expression that she was not buying his explanation and so he sprang to his feet and proceeded to lead the way along the path that would soon turn abruptly downward to follow the rocky gorge.

The group slowly made their way for about 90 minutes before coming to the first spot marked on the map as potentially dangerous. The descending trail ran straight down and narrowed to the degree that the four were forced to proceed cautiously downward in single file. In spite of her advanced age, Ohma remained in excellent physical condition and had little more difficulty negotiating the downward climb than her friends.

Soon the narrow formation gave way to a horizontal walkway strewn with boulders that had fallen from the surrounding walls. Ishim led the way, with Plabius next, followed by Ohma and lastly Nena. As they turned a corner, the four heard a noise from above and, in the blink of an eye, Plabius pushed past Ohma grabbing onto Nena's shirt sleeve, pulling her forward so that Nena ended up piled on top of Plabius and Ohma. The four covered their eyes to shield them from the dust that had been created by a huge boulder landing in the very spot where Nena had stood just seconds ago.

"Wow! That was a close call!" Ohma shouted.

"Thank you for saving my life, Plabius," Nena added. "I now see that the whole notion of security is really an illusion. I tried to avoid the greatest chance of danger by trailing the pack only to have it nearly smack me off the head!"

"What we resists persists, as the old slogan goes," Ishim laughed. "I suppose there is a lesson awaiting us at every turn."

"That is IF we choose to learn it," Ohma smiled.

As she spoke these words, three scorpion flying

stars went buzzing by Nena's head. The group looked back to see the guards they had evaded at the lake now gaining upon them in close pursuit.

"Come, quickly!" commanded Ishim.

The others headed his words and soon they were moving forward at a brisk pace along the narrow rock-hewn trail.

"Look out!" Nena shouted, lunging backward as she did.

Ohma looked up to see a huge rockslide descend upon their path, completely separating Plabius and Ishim from Nena and her. Within a few moments more, the guards plunged upon Nena and Ohma, taking them prisoner.

On the other side of the rock pile, Plabius and Ishim stood helplessly staring at each other in shock as the realization hit them simultaneously that they were now unable to rescue or even catch a glimpse of their friends.

Chapter 10

Nena's Lesson

Nena and Ohma shook the dust from their hair in unison. The nimble guards, determined not to be eluded again, tied their hands securely behind their backs.

Nena turned her head to face their attackers and as she did, her mouth dropped and tears welled in her eyes in disbelief.

"It's him!" shouted Nena's companion.

"Why, I know you!" she seethed to one of the guards. "You are Sargon. I will NEVER forget your face as long as I live. You're the man who killed my poor father!"

Nena's words were more powerful than any weapon. The guard fell backward as if hit by a blow to the head.

Slowly regaining his composure, Sargon spoke, "Why, you're the king's daughter! Only you're all grown up now."

"And you're the same evil man who killed a good-hearted and innocent man years ago!" Nena's companion retorted.

"Now, wait a minute. You've got it all wrong!" Sargon's companion reacted.

"That was an accident. I was just doing my job!" Sargon defended.

"Just like you're just doing your job now, I suppose!" Nena shot right back.

"That's right! How was he supposed to know that a crazy man dressed in rags setting fire to the castle was the king?" continued Sargon's companion.

"I was trying to SAVE the king from the actions of a deranged lunatic, not kill him!" Sargon explained. "It wasn't my fault! It was his."

"And what's your excuse now?" she mocked.

"I am following orders, as any good soldier will! Just following orders from my superiors," the guard countered. "Even after the accident, after I was cleared of all charges, I continued my loyalty to the leaders of our country."

"Even if those leaders are corrupt and unethical?" Nena demanded.

"They are still my leaders and superiors."

"He doesn't make the rules. He follows them," Sargon's companion added.

Ohma leaned closer to Nena. "My dear, it is clear that this man acts in accordance with his view of the world. Although we clearly do not condone his actions, we can understand them if we see things from his perspective," she whispered in a loving tone.

"But how can someone be so mixed up and take no responsibility for his actions?" Nena continued.

"To your way of reasoning, his logic is faulty. From his perspective, yours is!" Ohma explained. "It's up to you whether you are willing to allow someone like him the right to see things his own way."

"What about your rights?" Nena's companion asked her.

"But his thought process makes me so angry, Ohma!" Nena fumed.

"That is where you are not seeing things clearly, my dear. The guard thinks, speaks, and acts as he does. He does the best he can considering his perspective. You choose to be offended and upset by his opinions and actions," the wise old woman explained.

"But those actions affect us! How can we not care what he thinks and does?" Nena went on.

"My point is that we need not be at the mercy of what he or anyone else does or says. If you are angry, it is your choice, not his. If you decide to hate him and not forgive him, you suffer, not him. No one can make you feel anything without your permission," Ohma continued.

"But it's so juicy to hate!" Nena's companion interjected.

"So I am supposed to not care that he killed my father?" Nena wept.

"Of course, it is perfectly normal to mourn his loss and miss him. But to keep the anger in your heart about what happened, to wish another ill, to mistrust others because of bad experiences, harms you and those who love you and want you to be happy. Here is your choice: You can be right and indignantly angry about what happened so that it consumes your life energy and your peace of mind, ruins your health, robs you of your happiness, and keeps you suffering....or you can forgive him, heal and complete your past and move on with your life, and be happy. You can not be both angry and vengeful and happy at the same time. You must decide which is more important to you."

The guards lifted Nena and Ohma to their feet and shoved them forward along the path in the direction from which they had just come. "It's to the Detention Center for the two of you!" Sargon's partner shouted. "We know a shortcut by way of Level 5."

Nena and Ohma continued their conversation as they walked.

"So, Ohma, I understand what you are saying about putting the past behind us and forgiving those who hurt us," Nena went on. "But what if they continue to do bad things? Must you just accept them and continually forgive one abusive situation after another?"

"Do not misunderstand, my dear. I am not agreeing with abusive or hurtful behavior. We all have the right to avoid such insults and aggressions. I mean, it makes no sense to invite abuse by remaining in a bad situation. At the same time, we need not let the bad behavior of others infect our souls and sour our minds. If we can reason with them and be the source of their personal development and insights, great! If not, it is not our responsibility to get sucked into their dysfunction."

"I think I understand. So, you are saying that people do the best they know how to based upon the way they see things. We do not have to agree with or subject ourselves to their views. But when we allow them to ruin our happiness and consume our energy, it hurts us, not them."

"Exactly! You are so bright, my love!" Ohma congratulated Nena, smiling. "We can always take responsibility for living from the qualities that matter most to us, allowing others the space to be who they are. For when we give them the room to see the light, without forcing our perspective on them, they are more likely to learn, grow, and evolve in their thinking."

"I guess no one likes to be made wrong…even if they are!" Nena chuckled.

"The access to forgiveness is empathy, Nena," Ohma went on. "If we can ask ourselves 'What must they have been thinking to speak or act as they did?' we can gain insights into what it must be like in their world for them to do what they do."

"You know, Ohma, it is so freeing to forgive and give up my right to hate him. I feel like a huge burden has been lifted from my shoulders," Nena sighed in relief. "But I guess we still need to do our best to get out of the pickle we're now in!"

"Yes, dear. And we will have a much better chance of doing so if we are level-headed and not driven by hatred, anger, sadness, and fear," Ohma concluded.

The group continued along their path soon

reaching Level 7 of the Septropolis. This level was marked by a grand stone archway outlined in chiseled ancient lettering that read "Enter Here All Ye Who Long for Peace of Mind."

As they passed through the gateway, Ohma grabbed a flag that flanked the entrance. It read...

"FORGIVENESS IS A BLESSING THAT ENSURES HAPPINESS AND PEACE OF MIND."

Chapter 11

The Cave of Inspiration

Ishim and Plabius snapped out of the shocked state that had been created by the landslide and the subsequent capture of their friends.

“What do we do now?” Ishim asked.

“We need to find Ohma and Nena. I’m certain they are taking them to the Detention Center. Take a look at the map,” Plabius requested.

Ishim pulled the now badly wrinkled piece of parchment from his shirt. “It shows that the processing hub for the Detention Center lies on Level 7 of the Septropolis. From here, it looks like the fastest way to get to Level 7 is by way of a series of underground tunnels created in the building of the Septropolis. We’ll need to descend here and pass through this cave marked with an asterisk,” Ishim explained, pointing to the map.

“Why do you suppose that cave is marked that way?” Plabius asked.

“I expect that we will find out soon enough!” Ishim answered.

The two friends began their descent through the tunnels leading to Level 6. The tunnels were pitch black and they needed to light their way with torches they made from some building remnants they found in the mouth of the passage.

“This is taking forever!” Ishim complained.

“That’s the way it always is when you’re in a hurry to get somewhere, especially when it means saving some friends!" Plabius added.

After a few hours of making their way through the winding passage, the two saw a twinkling light emanating from an opening in the rock.

"That, my friend, I would bet is our famous cave!" Ishim asserted holding up the map in the torchlight to confirm his suspicion.

"Careful, from the looks of the light, it appears someone made it here before us," Plabius cautioned.

Ishim cautiously approached the cave's entrance, poking his head in just enough to see that the cave itself was empty.

"The light is coming from that passage high up on the cave's far wall," Plabius cautioned.

The two inched their way along the cave's right wall, finally coming to the far wall where a series of boulders had formed a natural staircase leading up to the lit passage.

"Wait here while I check it out first," offered Ishim courageously.

As Plabius looked up, Ishim made his way up the

rock wall until he could easily peer into the higher cave chamber. As he looked in, his eyes grew wide and his mouth opened in surprise.

"What is it?" Plabius whispered to him. But Ishim did not respond.

"Enter, my son!" came a warm invitation from deep within the chamber.

Ishim raised his torch to see a ghostly apparition seated on a throne flanked by two small torches.

"Who are you?" Ishim queried the specter cautiously.

"I am King Termaine," replied the spirit.

Plabius, sensing something important going on above in the chamber, had climbed up in Ishim's tracks and was now sharing in the grand spectacle taking place.

"How can that be?" Ishim asked. "King Termaine passed into shadow long ago."

"And that shadow sits before you now!" the phantom replied. "I have followed your valiant quest from the spirit world and as Ohma had prophesized long ago, I have come to this place to appear before you so that a great oversight might be remedied."

Plabius and Ishim watched silently as the renowned king of legend spoke.

"In my childhood, I first stumbled upon this cave and discovered these markings on its wall," the king explained.

Ishim and Plabius raised their torches toward the spot to which Termaine now pointed.

"It looks like I M I," Plabius suggested. "I've learned of the legend of your inspirational discovery from Nena, one of your noble descendants."

"That is what I also thought it said," the apparition continued. "And so I interpreted the message to mean "I am I" as in 'I am powerful, capable, confident, and empowered to do whatever I believe I can do."

"And that is your legacy as you empowered your people to believe in themselves and elevate their self-esteem," Ishim added.

"Yes, and I truly did and still do believe in the inherent magnificence of all people. It was by instilling such self-confidence among the people that they were emboldened to overthrow the oppressive tyrants in power before they overwhelmingly supported me as their choice for king, an honor I humbly accepted," Termaine went on.

"Your vision for the great subterranean city now called the Septropolis has also been manifest, Sire," Plabius added.

"That it has, but I envisioned it to be a great city that would protect my people from the dangers of invasion by all enemies, while becoming a model society that stands for freedom, justice, and self-direction, allowing all to live in peace, harmony, and abundance...everything essential for people to grow and prosper."

"How terrible it is that these ideals have now become corrupted by those who have assumed 'leadership' motivated by greed and with a hunger for power!" Ishim interrupted.

"Yes, we implemented many social programs including housing, health care, transportation, and established sound political structures to share the ruling power with a council and many levels of public servants, always for the common good of the people. My beloved daughter, Ohma, became my trusted minister. She instituted the Great Halls of Learning and implemented many of the programs I envisioned, while expanding upon my dream for a just and empowered society that would accomplish great things for the good of all."

"So, my lord, what went wrong?" Plabius asked, before listening intently for the king's answer.

"The answer was here all along on this very cave's wall. Take a good, close look," Termaine invited.

Plabius and Ishim approached the inscriptions on the wall. With their eyes fixated upon the painted letters, they could now see the inscription read "I M I_I" with the "_I" nearly fully obscured by the ravages of time.

"I don't understand, Sire," Ishim whispered, looking to the ghost for clarity.

"The true inscription read "I M I merged with U" –IMU – NOT "I M I alone! It was the YOU that I missed and failed to fully impress upon my people," the king confessed. "Sure, I got the message half right. That is I empowered them to believe in themselves and in their inherent magnificence. And they certainly were inspired to do great things…and at first with noble aspirations. But because I did not communicate to them the importance of taking their connection with their neighbor as seriously as their own empowerment, they became self-absorbed. They forgot that we are ALL connected so when we harm another, we harm ourselves!"

"That would explain the corruption and greed that spread throughout the leadership," Plabius added.

"Yes, self-esteem must include an appreciation for others, a genuine concern to do no harm while realizing fully what it is like to be another so that their rights and values are honored as we move our own visions forward. Without this piece, we created egotistical, selfish and power-hungry leaders who were willing to dishonor and violate the needs and rights of others just for personal gain and domination," he added. "It is now my request that you take this crucial message to the world in hope that we might set things right and avoid the impending doom that will inevitably result from greed, excess, and abuse of power."

"I promise we will, my lord," Ishim responded, bowing in homage to a great man.

"I just hope we are not too late!" Plabius added.

"All you can do is all you can do!" Termaine counseled. "Go with Godspeed now."

And with these words, the apparition vanished. In his place between the torches now flew a royal banner. It read...

"SELF-ESTEEM, NOT EGO, IS AN ESSENTIAL BLESSING REQUIRED FOR HAPPINESS AND FULFILLMENT IN ALL AREAS OF LIFE."

Chapter 12

The Detention Center

With their captors prodding them from behind, Nena and Ohma continued along their journey to the Detention Center located on Level 7 on the Septropolis. Although they were off to a fate uncertain and fraught with peril, Nena felt a newfound lightness in her heart. By forgiving the guard who had killed her father — the same man who was now putting her and Ohma directly in harm's way — a great burden had been lifted from her shoulders.

"This makes no sense, Ohma," Nena began.

"What's that, my dear?" Ohma asked.

"We are in the most dangerous predicament of our lives, possibly even marching off to our deaths, but I've never felt such an inner sense of peace since the day before my father died."

"That's wonderful, dear. That is the result of

knowing that all of life's experiences are for the good, even when it may not appear to be so in the moment. Non-attachment to an outcome is very freeing," Ohma went on.

"Yes, but my mind tells me that I should be more attached to how this all plays out for us all, Ohma. After all, people are dying!" Nena offered. "But my heart says trust that all will work out for the best, no matter what happens."

"Remember that death is only a change of state. No soul is ever lost. It is perfectly wonderful to be totally committed to the outcome you desire, like freeing the oppressed, saving your friends and yourself, and seeing that justice be done. But when we have little room to experience any challenges along the way, we lose our effectiveness and our personal power is diminished."

As Ohma finished these last words, the group passed a sign that read:

Entering Septropolis Detention Center Area.

Nena looked ahead and could see the tops of the tall guard towers rising above the massive stone walls that fortified the Detention Center's grounds.

As they prepared to enter the gate to the Detention Center, Sargon turned to Nena and spoke, "I wish things turned out differently for you. I'm truly sorry about your father. But you have to understand, it was NOT my fault!"

Nena smiled and replied, "I know you did the best you could and you did not mean to kill my father or cause me pain. I forgive you and wish you light and love."

Hearing these words, Sargon fell to his knees and cried, "I am so sorry."

"I'll take over with these new prisoners," ordered the guard stationed at the gate. "Return to your post and be on your way!" he barked his commands to Sargon and his partner, dismissing them.

The new guard escorted Nena and Ohma through the camp until they reached a stone holding pen labeled with a handwritten sign that read TRAITORS.

"In you go!" ordered the guard, cutting the

ties that bound their wrists while pushing his two new prisoners forward without regard for Ohma's age or Nena's feelings.

"Ohma!" several of the prisoners cried out in unison.

Ohma ran to embrace several of their fellow prisoners who she recognized as friends or colleagues. "Cyrit, Nanse, Jonah," Ohma cried out, as she embraced them one by one. "Nena, these are some of the former members of the Council who remained loyal to our vision and could not be bribed or corrupted."

"Jonah, Cyrit, and Nanse, meet my great great-granddaughter, Nena," as she made the introductions. "And I do mean doubly great!"

"It's an honor to meet you!" Nena responded. "Thank you for your commitment to doing the right thing."

"It's our honor," each responded in kind.

"How long have you been here?" Ohma asked.

"A little more than three weeks," Nanse replied, speaking for the others. "We were rounded up together and brought here to await our execution."

"We were rounded up along with the others you see here and labeled as enemies of the state by the leaders who took control of the Council," Jonah added.

Nena looked around to count 23 prisoners being held along with Ohma and herself.

"Won't we at least get a fair trial?" Nena asked.

"Oh, yes, at the end of a rope," Cyrit responded. "Same as the last group who met their fate earlier this week."

"It's hopeless!" Nanse added. "Our days are numbered."

"The only reason we have lived this long is because our captors have been more concerned with eradicating the Sumarians they've captured so far. They consider them to be the greater threat, I suppose," Cyrit added, pointing to an adjacent stone brig. That's where they keep those considered by many of the Council leaders to be a threat to human kind."

Nena turned to Ohma, "Surely, Ohma, with your gift of prophesy, you foresaw this dire situation!"

"My dear, although I have foreseen many a future happening, none are etched in stone. People always possess the free will to alter their futures and change their fates. Besides, what most would interpret as calamity is in the end, all for the good, as there is learning and evolvement in all lessons, even the most painful ones."

"Let us spend the hours we have left sharing our stories and exploring what possibilities we have available yet, if any," Jonah suggested.

And so they told their tales, and cried, and laughed, and shared their hopes and dreams, as they awaited their fate.

Empowered by their meeting with King Termaine's spirit, Plabius and Ishim now returned themselves to the task at hand...to find and rescue their friends and save the world from the consequences set in motion by the greedy and power-hungry renegade Council leaders.

"What does the map say about the path to the Detention Center?" Plabius asked.

"It looks like we must descend here and somehow make it through this gate undetected in order to gain access to both the area where they are probably holding our friends as well as to the place where our fellow Sumarians are likely awaiting their ends," Ishim explained. "Don't ask me how we can avoid their same fate, because I have no idea."

"One finds one's way by taking it!" Plabius declared. "So, let us be off on this most noble mission."

Ishim and Plabius began their difficult descent into the deepest of the Septropolis' levels. As they reached Level 7, they could feel the energy of the dark forces intensify. This is the area that the Council relegated to the most awful of practices. It is where they crafted and launched their evil plans, designed and tested their doomsday weapons, and murdered their adversaries. Because of the limited space and low ceiling, Plabius and Ishim were compelled to proceed more slowly and flying was all but impossible here.

"Look!" Ishim whispered. "There!" He pointed

to a man sitting by the side of the path, with his head in his hands.

"Why, that's Sargon, the guard who killed Nena's father and who captured Nena and Ohma. And he's sobbing!" Plabius whispered back in disbelief. "Let's approach him cautiously. It may be a ruse."

As the two Sumarians edged closer, Sargon paid no attention to the prior objects of his hunt.

Surrounding the guard, Ishim and Plabius pinned him to the ground, still expecting trickery. To their surprise, Sargon offered no resistance.

"Go ahead and kill me!" Sargon challenged. "I'm of no use to anyone anyways. My life has been a waste."

"He has messed up everything he ever did, even though he tried to do his job to the best of his ability," Sargon's companion added.

"Where are Ohma and Nena?" Plabius demanded, still pinning him to the ground.

"I've followed one terrible error with another, I'm afraid. I turned them over to the guards at the Detention

Center and they are certainly doomed now as well."

"I don't understand," Ishim challenged. "If you know you've erred, why did you turn them over to those who want them dead?"

"For years, I've tried my best to put that terrible day behind me…the day I killed my king. I thought that if I just focused on my duties as a good soldier, I could eventually forget about the horrible mistake I made that day. But by doing so, I have made yet another grievous error, one that will cost two more good people their lives," Sargon sobbed.

"He really deserves to die," Sargon's companion chimed in.

"Well, as I see it, you have a choice," Ishim interrupted. "You can sit here feeling forlorn and sorry for yourself, OR you can join us and help set things right, even now!"

Sargon raised his head. "It's hopeless. The Detention Center is surrounded by soldiers and no one has ever escaped from there, ever!"

"There's always a first time! Join us now and

let's set things right…or let us perish trying!" Plabius challenged the guard.

"You're right! Let us do what we can for good. It's about time for me, I'm afraid."

"Okay, so here's the plan…" whispered Ishim, huddling with Plabius and Sargon.

Sargon approached the gate to the Detention Center. "Did you process the prisoners I delivered to you a short while ago?"

"Of course!" answered the sentry. "They are securely in the brig."

"I have orders to interrogate them. They were traveling with two Sumarians who are highly dangerous and cunning," Sargon commanded.

"Very well, be quick about it. We'll be processing the lot very soon," the gate guard replied. "Here's the key."

As the sentry turned away, Sargon struck him in the

back of the neck, knocking him unconscious.

"Hurry, now!" he whispered and Ishim and Plabius sprang from their hiding places behind some rocks, joining Sargon as the three made their way to the stone structure where Nena, Ohma, and the other prisoners were being held.

"Nena, Ohma, it's us!" Plabius announced as Sargon turned the key in the lock. "Come quickly!"

In a flash Nena understood what was happening and turning to Ohma and the others, commanded "Come quickly, the hour of our liberation has come!"

The group, led by Sargon, Plabius, and Ishim, filed out the prison door.

"The other Sumarians are being held there," Nena instructed, pointing the adjacent structure out to Plabius and Ishim. Ishim grabbed the key from Sargon and in a flash swung open the iron door, liberating some 38 Sumarians trapped inside who had been just hours away from their executions.

"This way!" Sargon shouted. "There's a secret

lift that leads out of here and into the world above the Setropolis. But we must hurry, they will know of our plans too soon!"

As he spoke these words, a sentry high up in the watch tower spotted the escapees. "Escape! Escape!" he shouted, as he sounded a shrill alarm.

Within seconds chaos broke out. Soldiers from multiple positions lining the walls surrounding the camp let their arrows and spears fly, felling several Sumarians in their tracks.

"This way!" Sargon commanded, waving his arms for Nena, Ohma, and the others to follow.

As he looked up, Sargon saw that a guard had Nena directly in his sights. "Nena!" he yelled. As the guard let his arrow fly, Sargon lunged in front of Nena, taking the arrow intended for her in his chest.

Nena froze, momentarily in shock. The realization hit her like a bolt of lightning that the man she had hated for so many years had just given his own life to save hers.

"Make me proud, Nena!" Sargon cried out with his last breath.

"Come, Nena, we mustn't hesitate," Ohma implored. "Too many lives are at stake!"

"You go on, Ohma. Plabius, Ishim, and their comrades still need my help now!

"I foresaw this day long ago but it is nonetheless difficult to part from you now, my love," Ohma smiled, a tear welling up in her eye. "Take this, Nena, and promise me you will not read it until you are safe and sound in the Inner World."

"I promise and I love you, Ohma!" And with these words, Nena was gone, on her way to assist the Sumarians.

Ohma continued toward the lift that Sargon had pointed out moments ago. She led the way with the other former prisoners following closely behind to squeeze their way in.

The Sumarians trailing the pack were now engaged in a fierce battle with their persecutors. Many flew up and engaged in hand-to-hand combat with the guards who had lined the walls. Everywhere at the scene, the fleeing survivors witnessed the Sumarian heroes sacrificing their lives to buy time for those righteous leaders who had put their lives on the line for them by opposing the evil Council members.

"Plabius! Ishim!" Nena cried out. "Ohma and the others are safely gone. Let us gather your people and be off as well."

"Follow me!" Ishim cried out to those remaining. "We can still make it through the front gate. I saw a tunnel on the map that leads deep into the Inner World."

Plabius grabbed hold of Nena's arm and took flight behind Ishim, with the others following close behind. They flew close to the ground and within seconds, the group had left the gate, descended down the tunnel, and were off to reunite with those living safely in the Inner World.

As Nena had passed over the camp's fortified entrance, she grabbed hold of a flag with big red letters that read on one side "SARGON" flying at half-mast.

As she and Plabius hit the ground running to enter the escape tunnel, she unfurled it and together they glanced down at it. The other side read…

"THE GREATEST BLESSING OF ALL IS LOVE. THERE IS NO GREATER LOVE THAN TO LAY DOWN ONE'S LIFE FOR ANOTHER."

Chapter 13

Ohma's Prophesy

Within a few minutes, the lift had carried Ohma and the other former prisoners to an escape hatch outside Level 1 of the Septropolis. The builders of the subterranean city had constructed the large lift to facilitate their own escape in the event of a revolt by the city's inhabitants. Never had they envisioned it would be used to escape *from* them.

Warning sirens rang out throughout the Septropolis.

Nanse turned to Ohma and asked, "So, what now?"

"As long as we remain anywhere near the Septropolis or in the lands above near it, our lives will be in great peril. They will not rest until we are found!" Ohma said.

"But we must tell the world of the atrocities being committed in the name of the people!" Jonah interjected.

"And that we shall," Ohma assured. "But if we are killed, no one will know of the evil plans underway."

"Where can we go?" Cyrit wondered aloud.

"There is a place where no one will think to look. It is high up in the Red Rock Mountains. It is at quite a high elevation and not a very hospitable a place to live, but we should be safe there until we can spread the word to all and return to leadership in our world," Ohma continued.

"Let's put the plan to a vote," Jonah suggested.

"All in favor?" Nanse asked.

"Aye," went up the unanimous response from the group of 21.

"All opposed?" Nanse continued.

"Very well, we are off to our new temporary home high in the Red Rock Mountains," she concluded.

Word quickly spread throughout the ruling Council of what had transpired in the prisons of Level 7.

Zuavas, head of the renegade Council, called an emergency session of the ruling body.

Standing to address the governing body, he spoke, "We must act quickly! Soon word of the uprising will spread and embolden the people to revolution. The Sumarian situation will become known by all and the many bleeding hearts in favor of championing their rights will turn the masses against us. We must demand that our scientists move forward rapidly with their tests."

Chacum, second in command at the Council, stood up, "The only language that the foolish masses understand is absolute power. And the crystal experiments will unleash for us the awesome power to destroy any and all who oppose us. Let us have our scientists make ready the weapons that will safeguard our futures."

"That will teach them!" Chacum's shoulder companion added. "How dare they revolt!"

"Very well. Sentry, notify the scientists that they are to move the Doomsday Project forward with lightening speed. It's time we put these rebels in their place along with that Sumarian riffraff," Zuavas ordered.

After nearly a six-hour trek, Nena, Plabius, and Ishim finally arrived at their intended destination in the Inner World, leading the Sumarian refugees home at last.

"So, this is home!" Nena exclaimed with satisfaction. "I think I could get to like it here."

"That's good, because it may be a while until we can overthrow the evil Council and resume just rule in the Septropolis as well as in the World Above," Ishim replied.

"I hope Ohma and the others made it safely out,"

Nena worried.

"I'm certain they did," Plabius assured her. "We can get word to our friends in the World Above and they can get a message to Ohma and the others for us."

"Since we now safe and sound here in the Inner World, I suppose it is time for me to read Ohma's note," Nena shared nervously. "I've seen these notes from Ohma before. It is one of her prophesies."

Nena unfolded the note with her hands trembling as Plabius and Ishim looked on.

PRECIOUS NENA, MY DARLING DEAR
HERE COME THE WORDS YOU'LL DREAD TO HEAR
A CLEANSING CHANGE IS NEAR AT HAND
THE WORLD ABOVE WILL SOON DISBAND

THOUGH YOU MAY THINK THIS NEWS IS DIRE
KNOW FULL WELL THAT IT'S REQUIRED
WHEN GREED AND EVIL TIP THE SCALES
THE NEED FOR REBIRTH WILL PREVAIL

THOUGH CHANGE S THUS MAY MAKE YOU CRY
REMEMBER WELL THAT NOTHING DIES
FROM THE DELUGE WILL PREVAIL
NEW LIFE, NEW LOVE, NEW HOPE FOR ALL

SAFE YOU'LL BE WHERE LIFE IS GRAND
YOUR DESCENDANTS WILL NUMBER LIKE GRAINS OF SAND
I CHARGE YOU NOW WITH THIS COMMAND:
SPREAD THESE BLESSINGS THROUGHOUT YOUR LAND!

AND PEACE SHALL REIGN IN THE INNER WORLD
UNTIL THE LESSONS BECOME UNFURLED
LIKE THE CHERISHED WINDOW DRESSINGS
THE FLAGS REMIND ALL OF THEIR BLESSINGS

ABOUT ME, YOU MUST WORRY NOT
FOR IT IS JUST MY FATE, MY LOT
TO HELP THOSE HERE IN THE WORLD ABOVE
UNTIL THE LIGHT-BEARERS SPREAD THEIR LOVE

WITH LOVE AND LIGHT ALWAYS,
YOUR OHMA

Nena sat down upon the ground, at once shocked and stunned by Ohma's prophesy. "What do we do now?" she asked Plabius and Ishim.

"We do as Ohma instructed us to do. To worry not and to spread the Seven Blessings throughout the Inner World," Ishim replied.

"It's apparently too late to do much for the World Above, but we can do a lot right here in the Inner World. Our leadership will make the difference for all the people in the Inner World, no matter their race, their origin, or their special gifts," Plabius added.

"I am inspired and humbled by you both and I love you both dearly!" Nena wept.

"We are family now and together we shall spread the Seven Blessings until their news is firmly planted in the hearts of all!" Ishim continued.

He gathered the flags they had discovered along their journey.

"Nahua, you are the swiftest messenger of our people. Take these seven flags and see that a copy of each is hoisted high in every town and every cave, in every home, and for every heart to behold throughout our land. Also, find Ohma and present a copy of each to her so that she may fly them high for all to see and be inspired by the blessings readily available to us all," Ishim directed.

Chapter 14

The Red Rock Mountains

Ohma led her group past the shores of the Great Sea, past the golden plains and up the steep mountainside until at last they reached their final destination high in the Red Rock Mountains.

"The elevation is so high here that not much grows. But we will be safe from our persecutors, it will protect us from the coming changes, and we will learn to call this our home," Ohma declared, throwing down her walking stick and taking her seat upon a large flat rock.

"What changes and when will we come off this mountain top to warn the people of the Council members' evil deeds and lead them to establish a just rule for all?" Nanse asked as all the others numbering 21 in all looked on.

"I'm afraid that it is too late to right this ship. As we speak, the scientists are hard at work and the fruits of their labors will very soon spiral out of control, bringing about their own destruction and that of the World Above as we know it," Ohma prophesied.

"You said we will be safe here. How will we not perish as well?" Jonas asked.

"When you awaken tomorrow, the world will be renewed. Many lands will rise while others will fall. The Great Sea will run dry. New rivers will arise from it throughout the Inner World. A parched desert will remain in its stead. We will be safe and dry here on this mountaintop," Ohma continued.

"So, life will go on as we know it?" Cyrit interrupted.

"Life will go on, although not as we know it. The sun will be obscured and a dark shadow shall envelope the Earth. But fear not, we will survive and make do and we will be grateful as we count our blessings and await the lessons or renewal that will be spread by the light-bearers to come!"

Ohma paused for a moment to survey the troubled looks upon her new family's faces. As she caught her breath, the group could see a man and a young girl walking slowly up the path from which the group had recently come.

"Fear not, for they are not our adversaries," Ohma instructed, awaiting their arrival.

In a few minutes, the newcomers had arrived at the mountain top site.

"Welcome, friends! I have been expecting you!" Ohma called out. The group momentarily turned their gaze from the new visitors back to Ohma, marveling at her clairvoyance.

"I am Costas and this is my little darling daughter,

Matilda," the man called out. "We are on a mission for my dear wife, the great healer Tonesia, in search of healing herbs."

"I am called the Auger," Ohma replied. "Welcome to our family. I have been told that a great adventure awaits you in years to come, Miss Matilda."

Matilda looked at her father for an explanation of what this strange lady meant, but none was forthcoming.

And so Costas and Matilda learned the story of their new friends' daring escape as they shared their stories in kind. The Auger knew that Costas was soon to lose his home and, much more importantly, Tonesia, the love of his life and the most important part of his world; Matilda would likewise lose her loving mother. Still, the Auger knew that the time had passed to avoid the events that were only a few short hours away.

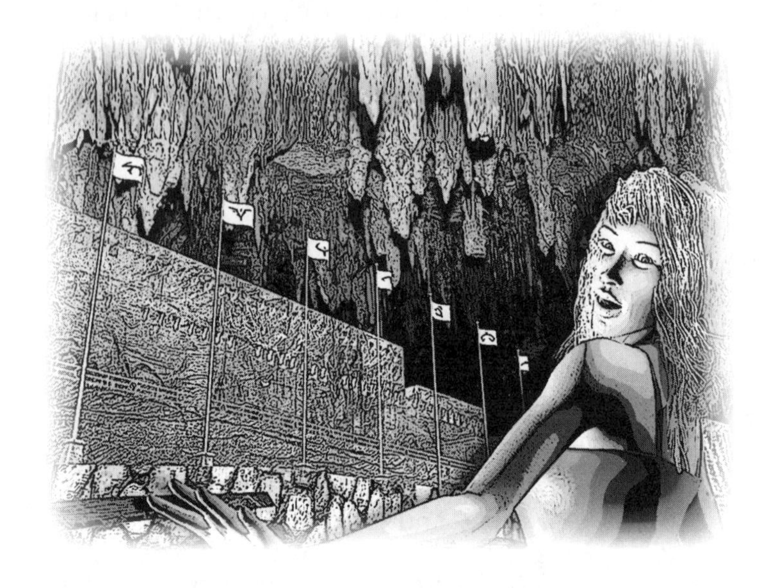

Chapter 15

Epilog

Just as the Auger had foretold, the night was filled with the clamor of massive disruptions. The scientists, under orders to move their tests ahead with extreme velocity under the threat of death by the evil Council members if they refused, threw caution to the wind. Their efforts to harness the awesome power of the doomsday weapons that were developing backfired. With the massive release of raw energy that was unleashed deep within Level 7 of the Septropolis, the Earth's plates shifted. The Great Seas emptied into new rivers that ran deep into the Earth, drowning the inhabitants of the World Above as well as those living in the Septropolis at the same time.

The lands of the Inner World were greatly expanded and the geography of that world grew more varied and increased in size. Many new races were formed as a result of the radiation released by the new weaponry out of control.

True to her word, the Auger taught her clan the skills they would need to survive in the harsh new environment deprived of light that had been created by the dark forces.

The morning after the great cataclysm, the residents of the Red Rock Mountains arose to see seven multicolored banners flapping in the dry wind. They read:

sion that passionately inspires you to be your best, to contribute your gifts to others, and makes your life happy and fulfilled is a true blessing.

Empathy for what it is like in your neighbor's world is a true blessing.

Unselfish contribution to the lives of others is a sacred blessing.

Every person is blessed with a multitude of unique gifts. The choice is yours to be grateful and make the most of these blessings or focus instead on all your petty concerns.

Forgiveness is a blessing that ensures happiness and peace of mind

---

Self-esteem, not ego, is an essential blessing required for happiness and fulfillment in all areas of life.

The greatest blessing of all is love. There is no greater love than to lay down one's life for another.

Flags displaying these blessings flew prominently from their new mountain top home and their message brought hope to the people who would have likely perished without their guidance and inspiration.

Through all of her learning experiences, Nena learned to reinterpret her past. She was no longer plagued by the nagging fear that she had created in her mind, namely that men hurt you, leave you, and can't be trusted. Nena and Plabius' love for each other grew and they were soon wed. As Ohma had predicted, they were blessed by many children whose offspring likewise multiplied to be more numerous than the sands of the seashore.

Shortly after their return to the Inner World, Ishim met a wonderful Sumarian girl. They fell in love and were likewise blessed by a large and prolific family.

Nena, Plabius, and Ishim spent their remaining days traveling to the ends of the newly formed lands of the Inner World, teaching and spreading the Seven Blessings that had so impacted their own lives. Nena grew in love and self-esteem as well as in her commitment to others. Nena eventually found herself able to ignore her shoulder companion more frequently. Over time, her companion gradually shrunk in size, her negative chatter grew quiet and and eventually the gremlin disappeared altogether.

True to Ohma's prophesy, the peace the three friends championed in their world lived on until their descendants lost sight of the importance of spreading the Seven Blessings. True to the pattern long established by history, greed and selfishness eventually replaced love and contribution as self-interest and ego made a comeback... and the world became once again in need of a new dose of love and light. But, that of course, is where Matilda's quest began and the substance of yet another installment in the Legends of Light.

The End

About the Author

Dr. Joe Rubino is widely acknowledged as one of the world's foremost experts on self-esteem elevation. He is also a top success and productivity coach and the CEO of The Center for Personal Reinvention. To date more than 2 million people have benefited from his coaching, self-esteem elevation and leadership development training. The Center provides coaching, productivity, self-esteem and leadership development courses that champion people to maximize their personal power and effectiveness to live their best lives.

Please visit the following websites to learn more about Dr. Rubino's life-impacting programs:

- **http://www.CenterForPersonalReinvention.com**
- **http://www.TheSelfEsteemBook.com**
- **http://www.SuccessCodeSystem.com**
- **http://www.cprsuccess.com/selfesteemsystem.html**

Dr. Rubino is the author of 10 best-selling books, 2 video and 5 audio programs available worldwide in 23 languages and in 53 countries. These include:

- *The Magic Lantern: A Fable about Leadership, Personal Excellence, and Empowerment*
- *The Legend of the Light-Bearers: A Fable about Personal Reinvention and Global Transformation*
- *The Self-Esteem Book: The Ultimate Guide to Boost the Most Underrated Ingredient for Success and Happiness in Life*
- *The Success Code: 29 Principles for Achieving Maximum Abundance, Success, Charisma, & Personal Power in Your Life*
- *The Success Code: More Authentic Power Principles for Living Intentionally, Book II*

Also by Dr. Joe Rubino:

- *Secrets of Building a Million Dollar Network Marketing Organization from a Guy Who's Been There, Done That and Shows You How You Can Do It Too*
- *The 7-Step System to Building a $1,000,000 Network Marketing Organization: How to Achieve Financial Freedom through Network Marketing*
- *The Ultimate Guide to Network Marketing Success*
- *10 Weeks to Network Marketing Success – CD Album plus Workbook*
- *Secret #1 – Self-Motivation Audible and Subliminal Affirmation CDs*
- *15 Secrets Every Network Marketer Must Know*

To request information about any of The Center for Personal Reinvention's programs or to order any of Dr. Rubino's books, visit:

- **http://www.CenterForPersonalReinvention.com**

Recommended Personal Development Programs

The Center for Personal Reinvention

Dr. Joe Rubino and Dr. Tom Ventullo

Where are you stopped in your life and in your business?
Where is there an unacceptable level of resignation or conflict?
Where are there interpersonal listening and communications skills lacking?
Where is there a missing in terms of partnership, commitment and vision?

The world we live and work in is marked by unprecedented change and fraught with new and complex challenges. For many of us, life begins to look like an uphill struggle to survive instead of a fun and exciting opportunity to grow, risk, and play full out in partnership with others. The stresses, conflicts and frustrations we experience daily need not be so.

In place of these, there exists another possibility.

...To live and work in choice -- empowered by the challenges of life.

...To champion others to achieve excellence in a nurturing environment that fosters partnerships.

...To acquire the success principles that support mutuality, creativity and harmony.

...To take on the art of listening and communicating in such a way that others are impacted to see new possibilities for accomplishment, partnership and excellence.

Reinventing ourselves, our relationships and our perception of the world is the result of a never ending commitment to our own personal magnificence and to that of others. It is made possible through the acquisition of approximately 50 key principles that cause people to begin to view life and people in an entirely different way. When people really ***get*** these principles, life, relationships, and new possibilities for breakthroughs show up from a totally fresh perspective. Through the use of cutting edge technology as a vibrant basis for learning, growing and acting, The Center For Personal Reinvention is successful in shifting how life shows up for people by supporting them to self-discover these life-changing principles.

With this program, YOU will:

- Uncover the secrets to accessing your personal power while maximizing your productivity.
- Gain clarity on exactly what it will take to reach your goals with velocity.
- Create a structure for skyrocketing your effectiveness while developing new and empowering partnerships.
- Learn how taking total responsibility for every aspect of your life and business can result in breakthrough performance.
- Discover what the key elements are to a detailed action plan and how to reach your goals in record time.
- Acquire the keys to listening and communicating effectively and intentionally.
- Recognize and shift out of self-defeating thoughts and actions.
- Gain the insight to better understand others with new compassion and clarity.
- Learn how to develop the charisma necessary to attract others to you.
- Experience the confidence and inner peace that comes from stepping into leadership.

The Center for Personal Reinvention

...Bringing people and companies back to life!

Customized Courses and Programs Personally
Designed For Achieving Maximum Results

Areas of Focus include:

Designing Your Future
Making Life and Businesses Work
Generating Infinite Possibilities
Creating Conversations For Mutuality
Commitment Management
Personal Coaching and Development
Maximizing Personal Effectiveness
Breakthrough Productivity
Leadership Development
Relationship and Team Building
Conflict Resolution
Listening For Solutions
Systems For Personal Empowerment
Personal and Productivity Transformation
Designing Structures for Accomplishment
Creating Empowered Listening Attitudes
Possibility Thinking
Forwarding Action
Structures For Team Accountability
Innovative Thinking
Completing With The Past
Creating a Life Of No Regrets

The Center for Personal Reinvention champions companies and individuals to achieve their potential through customized programs addressing specific needs consistent with their vision for the future.

Contact us today to explore how we might impact your world!

The Center for Personal Reinvention
PO Box 217,
Boxford, MA 01921

DrJoe@DrJoeRubino.com

Tel: (888) 821-3135
Fax: (630) 982-2134

Books by Dr. Joe Rubino

The Magic Lantern:

A Fable about Leadership, Personal Excellence and Empowerment

Set in the magical world of Center Earth, inhabited by dwarves, elves, goblins, and wizards, *The Magic Lantern* is a tale of personal development that teaches the keys to success and happiness. This fable examines what it means to take on true leadership while learning to become maximally effective with everyone we meet. Renowned personal development trainer, coach, and veteran author, Dr. Joe Rubino tells the story of a group of dwarves and their young leader who go off in search of the secrets to a life that works, a life filled with harmony and endless possibilities and void of the regrets and upsets that characterize most people's existence. With a mission to restore peace and harmony to their village in turmoil, the characters overcome the many challenges they encounter along their eventful journey. Through self-discovery, they develop the principles necessary to be the best that they can be as they step into leadership and lives of contribution to others.

The Magic Lantern teaches us:

- the power of forgiveness
- the meaning of responsibility and commitment
- what leadership is really all about
- the magic of belief and positive expectation
- the value of listening as an art
- the secret to mastering one's emotions and actions
- and much more.

It combines the spellbinding storytelling reminiscent of Tolkien's *The Hobbit* with the personal development tools of the great masters.

The Legend of the Light-Bearers:

A Fable about Personal Reinvention and Global Transformation

Is it ever too late for a person to take on personal reinvention and transform his or her life? Can our planet right itself and reverse centuries of struggle, hatred and warfare? Are love, peace, and harmony achievable possibilities for the world's people? *The Legend of the Light-Bearers* is a tale about vision, courage, and commitment, set in the magical world of Center Earth. In this much anticipated prequel to Dr. Joe Rubino's internationally best-selling book, *The Magic Lantern: A Fable about Leadership, Personal Excellence and Empowerment,* the process of personal and global transformation is explored within the guise of an enchanting fable. As the action unfolds in the world following the great Earth Changes, this personal development parable explores the nature of hatred and resignation, the secrets to transformation, and the power of anger and the means to overcoming it and replacing it with love. It shows what can happen when people live values-based lives and are guided by their life purposes instead of their destructive moods and their need to dominate others. If ever our world needed a roadmap to peace and cooperation and our people, a guide to personal empowerment and happiness, they do now...and this is the book.

The Self-Esteem Book:

The Ultimate Guide to Boost the Most Underrated Ingredient for Success and Happiness in Life

With this book YOU will:

- Uncover the source of your lack of self-esteem
- Heal the past and stop the downward spiral of self-sabotage
- Replace negative messages with new core beliefs that support your happiness and excellence
- Realize the secret to reclaiming your personal power
- See how you can be strong and authentic. Use your vulnerability as a source of power
- Design a new self-image that supports your magnificence
- Realize the power of forgiveness
- Discover the secret to un upset-free life
- Re-establish your worth and reinvent yourself to be your best
- Create a vision of a life of no regrets

To order your Ultimate Self-Esteem Pack including

The Self-Esteem Book, visit:

- **http://www.TheSelfEsteemBook.com**

The Success Code:

29 Principles for Achieving Maximum Abundance, Success, Charisma, and Personal Power in Your Life

What exactly distinguishes those who are effective in their relationships, productive in business and happy, powerful, and successful in their approach to life from those who struggle, suffer, and fail? That is the key question that *The Success Code* explores in life-changing detail. The information, examples, experiences, and detailed exercises offered will produce life-altering insights for readers who examine who they *are being* on a moment-to-moment basis that either contributes to increasing their personal effectiveness, happiness and power — or not. As you commit to an inquiry around what it takes to access your personal power, you will gain the tools to overcome any challenges or limiting thoughts and behavior and discover exactly what it means to be the best you can be.

With this book YOU will:

- Uncover the secrets to accessing your personal power.
- Create a structure for maximizing your effectiveness with others.
- Learn to take total responsibility for everything in your life.
- Discover the key elements to accomplishment and how to reach your goals in record time.
- Identify your life rules and discover how honoring your core values can help you maximize productivity.
- Complete your past and design your future on purpose.
- Discover the keys to communicating effectively and intentionally.
- Stop complaining and start doing.
- Seize your personal power and conquer resignation in your life.
- Learn how to generate conversations that uncover new possibilities.
- See how embracing problems can lead to positive breakthroughs in life.
- Leave others whole while realizing the power of telling the truth.
- Learn how to develop the charisma necessary to attract others to you

The Success Code:

More Authentic Power Principles for Living Intentionally, Book II

This revealing book continues where The Success Code, Book I left off with more powerful insights into what it takes to be most happy, successful and effective with others.

With this book YOU will:

- Discover the keys to unlock the door to success and happiness.
- Learn how your listening determines what you attract to you.
- And how to shift your listening to access your personal power.
- See how creating a clear intention can cause miracles to show up around you.
- Learn the secrets to making powerful requests to get what you want from others.
- Discover how to fully connect with and champion others to realize their greatness.
- Learn to create interpretations that support your excellence and avoid those that keep you small.

- Develop the power to speak and act from your commitments.
- See how communication with others can eliminate unwanted conditions from your life.
- Discover the secret to being happy and eliminating daily upsets.
- Learn how to put an end to gossip and stop giving away your power.
- Develop the ability to lead your life with direction and purpose and discover what it's costing you not to do so.
- And More!!

Dr. Joe Rubino's personal development book series is a powerful course in becoming the person you wish to be. Read these books, take on the success principles discussed and watch your life and business transform and flourish.

THE 7-Step Success System to Building a Million Dollar Network Marketing Dynasty:

How to Achieve Financial Independence through Network Marketing

This book is perhaps the most comprehensive step-by-step guide ever written on how to build a lasting, multi-million dollar organization. *Success Magazine* called Master Instructor, Dr. Joe Rubino a Millionaire Maker in their landmark We Create Millionaires cover story because of his ability to pass along the power to achieve top-level success to others. Now you can learn exactly how Dr. Joe built his own dynasty so that you can too. Follow the 7 detailed steps-to-success blueprint and join the ranks of network marketing's top income earners.

Step 1:	Visioning — Establish Your Reasons for Joining & Create a Compelling Vision
Step 2:	Planning —Create a Master Plan That Will Support You to Realize Your Vision
Step 3:	Prospecting —Effective Prospecting: Who, Where, and How and How Many?
Step 4:	Enrolling —The Power to Enroll: How to Become an Enrollment Machine
Step 5:	Training —Train like a Master Instructor: Structures for Successful Partnerships
Step 6:	Personal Development —Grow as Fast as Your Organization Does: Create Structures for Personal Excellence
Step 7:	Stepping Into Leadership — The Keys to Developing Other Self-Motivated Leaders

The Ultimate Guide to Network Marketing:

37 Top Network marketing Income-Earners Share Their Most Preciously-Guarded Secrets to Building Extreme Wealth

In *The Ultimate Guide to Network marketing,* Dr. Joe Rubino presents a wide variety of proven business-building techniques and tactics taken from thirty-seven of the most successful network marketers and trainers in the industry. Together, these thirty-seven experts present a comprehensive resource for the specialized information and strategies that network marketers need to grow their businesses and achieve top-level success.

The three primary elements of successful network marketing are prospecting, following up, and enrolling. Here, you'll find a unique blend of expert opinion and practical advice on how to be more successful at these vital tasks. This invaluable resource lets you explore the many various effective tactics and techniques the contributors used to make their fortunes—so you can pick what works best for you.

Inside, you'll find unbeatable advice on these topics and many more:

- Crafting a winning attitude that attracts others
- Mastering the art of persuasion
- Instant changes that make you more believable when speaking
- Identifying a prospect's most important values
- Simple, valuable skills you should teach your team
- Tactics for convincing skeptical and reluctant prospects
- How to work the "cold" market for prospects
- Seven profitable Internet prospecting tools
- Prospecting at home parties, trade shows, and fairs
- Direct mail prospecting tips
- How to become a great leader

Revealing a world of secrets it would take a lifetime in the industry to amass, *The Ultimate Guide to Network marketing* is a one-of-a-kind resource that will put you on the inside track to success. Loaded with hard-earned wisdom and essential techniques, it will advise your every step as you build your network marketing business.

Secrets Of Building A Million Dollar Network Marketing Organization From A Guy Who's Been There Done That And Shows You How To Do It Too.

Learn the Keys to Success in Building Your Network-Marketing Business - From the Man Success Magazine called a "Millionaire Maker" in their Cover Story.

With This Book You Will:

- Get the 6 keys that unlock the door to success in network marketing.
- Learn how to build your business free from doubt and fear.
- Discover how the way you listen has limited your success. And ...
- Accomplish your goals in record time by shifting your listening.
- Use the Zen of Prospecting to draw people to you like a magnet.
- Build rapport and find your prospect's hot buttons instantly.

- Pick the perfect prospecting approach for you.
- Turn any prospect's objection into the very reason they join.
- Identify your most productive prospecting sources. And ...
- Win the numbers game of network marketing.
- Develop a step-by-step business plan that ensures your future.
- Design a Single Daily Action that increases your income 10 times.
- Rate yourself as a top sponsor and business partner.
- Create a passionate vision that guarantees your success.
- And More!!!

10 Weeks to Network-Marketing Success:

The Secrets to Launching Your Very Own Million-Dollar Organization in a 10-Week Business-Building and Personal-Development Self-Study Course

Learn the business-building and personal-development secrets that will put you squarely on the path to network-marketing success. *10 Weeks to Network-Marketing Success* is a powerful course that will grow your business with velocity and change your life!

With this course, YOU will:

- Learn exactly how to set up a powerful 10-week action plan that will propel your business growth.
- Learn how to prospect in your most productive niche markets.
- Discover your most effective pathways to success.
- Learn how to persuasively influence your prospects by listening to contribute value.
- Build your business rapidly by making powerful requests.
- Discover the secret to acting from your commitments.

- Create a powerful life-changing structure for personal development.
- See the growth that comes from evaluating your progress on a regular basis.
- Learn how listening in a new and powerful way will skyrocket your business.
- Uncover the secret to accepting complete responsibility for your business.
- Learn how to transform problems into breakthroughs.
- Develop the charisma that allows you to instantly connect with others on a heart-to-heart level.
- Identify the secrets to stepping into leadership and being the source of your success.
- And much more!

The *10 Weeks to Network-Marketing Success* Program contains 10 weekly exercises on 4 CDs plus a 37-page workbook.

15 Secrets Every Network Marketer Must Know-

Essential Elements and Skills Required to Achieve 6 & 7 Figure Success in Network Marketing

By Dr. Joe Rubino and John Terhune

Written by two of the top experts in network marketing, this book shares with readers 15 key principles which are the core secrets to network marketing success. The principles, strategies and tactics presented in this book will help network marketers maximize their personal effectiveness, attitude, and behavior as they build their dynasties. Based on proven, time-tested strategies and the long experience of two well-known and extremely well-qualified authors, this guide is an indispensible tool to support top network marketing achievement.

SECRET #1 - SELF MOTIVATION

Utilize The Latest in ***Whole Brain Inner Talk™*** Technology to take a trip to a deeper dimension of power within yourself and tap into The Most Important Secret To Success In Network Marketing... **SELF-MOTIVATION!**

Thought Modification Made Easy Audio CD Series

Put to work for you the powerful combination of the latest in patented and scientifically proven audible and subliminal brain wave technology developed by Dr. Eldon Taylor, the world's foremost expert on offsetting negative information by inputting positive messages directly into the subconscious. This safe and highly effective proven technology has been independently researched at leading institutions such as Stanford University. For the first time ever, this technology has been combined with the 124 thought altering positive self-talk affirmations developed by Dr. Joe Rubino, one of North America's foremost business trainers and coaches- the man Success Magazine called a “Millionaire Maker”. The result is a remarkable audio CD series that will give you the power to alter any limiting thoughts…The power to maximize your personal effectiveness to rapidly build your MLM business on purpose and with confidence.

This revolutionary two CD set consists of one Inner-Talk Program, which combines audible affirmations with the shadowed subliminal Inner Talk® affirmations, and one Ozo self-motivation program. Use the first at least once a day playing it in the background in your car or while you work or play. Use the second with headphones when you can take 20 minutes and close your eyes. The special frequencies will entrain brain wave activity and produce an optimal state for learning and conditioning new patterns, energizing you into action and filling your being with total confidence. It's like hiring Dr. Joe Rubino as your personal success coach!

Vision Works Publishing
PO Box 217
Boxford, MA 01921

To Order any of Dr. Joe Rubino's Life-Impacting Books or Audio Programs, Visit:

- **http://www.CenterForPersonalReinvention.com**

Call (888) 821-3135
Fax: (630) 982-2134

Email: VisionWorksBooks@Email.com

QUANTITY DISCOUNTS AVAILABLE